P9-ART-830

The Family Interrupted

ELOY URROZ

THE FAMILY INTERRUPTED

A Novel

Translated by Ezra E. Fitz

 **DALKEY ARCHIVE PRESS**

FRANKLIN COUNTY LIBRARY
906 NORTH MAIN STREET
LOUISBURG, NC 27549
BRANCHES IN BUNN,
FRANKLINTON, & YOUNGSVILLE

Previously published in Spanish as *La Familia Interrumpida* in 2011

© 2011 by Eloy Urroz
Translation copyright © 2011 by Ezra Fitz

First edition, 2016
All rights reserved

Library of Congress Cataloging-in-Publication Data

Names: Urroz Kanan, Eloy, 1967- author. | Fitz, Ezra E., translator.
Title: The family interrupted / by Eloy Urroz ; translated by Ezra Fitz.
Other titles: Familia interrumpida. English
Description: First edition. | Victoria, TX : Dalkey Archive Press, 2016.
Identifiers: LCCN 2015040721 | ISBN 9781564787330 (pbk. : acid-free paper)
Classification: LCC PQ7298.31.R73 F3613 2016 | DDC 863/.64--dc23
LC record available at http://lccn.loc.gov/2015040721

ILLINOIS
ARTS
COUNCIL
AGENCY

Partially funded by the Illinois Arts Council, a state agency

La presente traducción fue realizada con apoyo del Programa de Apoyo la Traducción de Obras Mexicanas en Lenguas Extranjeras (ProTrad)

This translation was carried out with the support of the Program to Support the Translation of Mexican Works into Foreign Languages (ProTrad)

Dalkey Archive Press
Victoria, TX / McLean / Dublin
www.dalkeyarchive.com

Dalkey Archive Press books are, in part, mad possible through the support of the University of Houston-Victoria and its programs in creative writing, publishing, and translation.

Typesetting: Mikhail Iliatov
Cover: Art by Eric Longfellow

Printed on permanent/durable acid-free paper in the United States of America

To the memory of my nephew Marcelo

For Antonio, Raquel, and Luciano

Everything will come down with you, like tinsel streamers once the party's over, even the shadow of a few days that lingered a while in music, and no one else will be able to evoke for the world what ends in the world with you. Pitiful? For you, maybe. But you're nothing more than one more card in the game, and it, though it hurts to acknowledge it, is not played by you or for you, but with you and for an instant.
— Luis Cernuda

There is no history of mankind, there is only an indefinite number of histories of all kinds of aspects of human life ... A concrete history of mankind, if there were any, would have to be the history of all men. It would have to be the history of all human hopes, struggles, and sufferings. For there is no one man more important than any other. Clearly, this concrete history cannot be written. We must make abstractions, we must neglect, select. But with this we arrive at the many histories ...
— Karl Popper

"I've done with it all. It's time I was dead."

"Well, that's a good one!" said Shtcherbatsky, laughing; "why, I'm only just getting ready to begin."

"Yes, I thought the same not long ago, but now I know I shall soon be dead."
— Tolstoy

1

"I'd like to see your eyes again."

He read the email, the short, succinct message. One, two, three, four times. It was so brief he could have reread it a hundred times a minute. But why? The message was as bright and clear as the solid screen on which he read and reread it, thoughtful and surprised. A girl signed it; or rather, nobody did. It was, in fact, unsigned. He simply gathered that it was a woman because the email address read rosasetefilla@yahoo.com. So he immediately supposed or surmised that the Christian name must be Rosa, yes, but it could have been any other. Still perplexed and mildly intrigued, he toyed with his colorful cup of Turkish coffee, turning it with his hand like a top. Was this a joke? Who the hell was Rosa Setefilla or whatever her name was? Where was she from? And why did she want to see him again, specifically his eyes? What was so special about them? He was fairly certain he had never met anyone named Rosa, let alone someone with such a mysterious surname, he thought, lost in the warmth emanating from the tiny cup in his hands; nevertheless, a second later, he corrected himself: at some point in his life, he must have crossed paths with someone with a name like that, because Setefilla sounded like something, something distant, something indistinguishable or spurious. It was just a hunch, barely even a tingle. But was it actually a woman? Couldn't it just as easily be a man? But who? All things considered, the fact is that he didn't have the slightest idea, try as he might on that afternoon, that hour and a half left there in New York, since (he confirmed, looking through his window) the night or pale twilight was breaking in the distance, a sort of purplish darkness in the soft pubic beard of atmosphere trimmed by the Manhattan skyline.

He lit a cigarette, crossed his legs, and thought for a while longer, still gazing out the window.

2

To understand (or observe) a war like the Spanish Civil War or the Mexican Revolution or any other war for that matter, with their millions or more dead, with their raging insanity and terror, with the many thousands of dead children, their bitterness and misfortune, their hundreds of thousands of little deaths and exiles with living parents and grandparents left behind, with young people being shot or tortured. To understand (or observe) their fright and pain, the incalculable stupidity and myopia, you have to move from the particular to the general and never, never work in the opposite direction, for unfortunately infamy can't be understood in reverse. You can't perceive — much less wring out — in reverse that which would otherwise cleave flesh, cut to the marrow of the soul, the spinal cord ... that which would otherwise endure a lifetime of lamentations and shame. Shame above all.

Perhaps all that can be perceived (and barely so) is the particular, the minimum, the atomic, the lowest, the infinitesimal. Conversely, it's impossible. Conversely, raging insanity and fear are lost or distorted, the pain is confounded or it contracts. It contracts. This, then, is a small history of the particular, the *very* particular, the *most* particular of all. And it's also about the children that Luis and Luis didn't have, and about the children that each of them lost. And that, precisely, is the only story that matters in this world (this speck of dust that's called a world) where the general is misleading or deceptive, dissipating into the atmosphere like droplets of camphor, like tawny tears. Expansiveness is always an abstraction, a pure conjecture elaborately smudged by facts and figures which, truth be told, nobody understands and which do not say (much less wring out) anything to anyone.

The truth is that Luis Salerno Insausti, a Mexican living in self-imposed exile in New York, *did not always know* that he *wouldn't* have children; once, as a young adolescent, he dreamed he was a parent, imagined himself the father of a three- or four-year-old boy, or, who knows, ten or eleven. A handsome, dark-skinned, happy, intelligent boy. But when did he dream this? He didn't know for sure, though he spent a long, long time on it. That happiness was an ancient one, with no exact date. However, with great effort and much regret, he was beginning to learn the opposite. He surmised, nearly around the same time, that he had discovered his new (mysterious) secret, his difference, his homosexuality: bit by bit, he was beginning to feel that he preferred men (or some men) over women, or that women (the most beautiful women) were simply less pleasing to him ... much less pleasing than some men. Nevertheless, this happened in a gradual, imperceptible way, even to himself, despite his desire to be ever attentive to everything going on around him. The bitterness, he knew now, was also gradual. But it never caught him unawares.

If memory serves, the contentious discovery or premonition that he was not to become a father (nobody would call him Dad in this world or speck of dust) came on the heels of that *other* revelation: his homosexuality, his gayness, his limp-wristedness, as Jacinto, his best friend, would say, despite having had no real idea about it before leaving for New York. But ... what was *that*, what did it mean to be gay or effeminate or faggoty or queer or whatever if he'd never slept with a man? Do you just realize it, all of a sudden? Do you perhaps feel something different? And where or how is it felt? Was it an unreachable itch caused by an imagined sting? Did you first have to actually sleep with a gay man to become one, or is it enough to just wake up one day, any day, and like a man more than a woman?

All things considered, the knowledge that he'd have no child was, and continued to be for years, the most ruinous of all discoveries, truly the most atrocious, the only one that counted when it all came down to it: he would not become a father, nobody would call him "Dad" despite the fact that deep down, and as contradictory as it might seem, he had, deeply entrenched, the most nefarious ideas about what this world, this Leviathan, could offer a newborn child in the twenty-first century.

3

Living in the Vullioni's house in Oxfordshire was almost worse than living hunkered down in a trench, scarcely moving for fear of being cut down by pro-Franco gunfire. Every passing day became more bitter and grim for Luis, hour after hour in that narrow little bourgeois house, with an unknown couple he didn't know in the least and whose mannerisms trended toward the strange and alien and who, moreover, didn't speak a word of Spanish. He was, as they say, trapped there in that borrowed bedroom, on that creaky borrowed floor, in another country whose language he did not speak, trying not to cough, not to scratch himself, not to move around too much (not even to go to the bathroom) so as not to be noticed, so he could become invisible to that English couple. And all because of that idiot Stanley, who would never discern let alone understand his complicated interior; all because of or thanks to that mannered little Englishman whom he hated now more than ever, especially since — either through him or his powerful godmother — he'd found himself stuck (up to his ears, this time) in this sad, god-awful mess: taking care of Basque children exiled in Great Britain, transplants like him, isolated like he was, desperate and helpless, as nostalgic for their homeland and families as he, Cernuda, thirty-six years of age, just *nel mezzo del cammin*. Who would have thought? But almost immediately he began to reconsider, still lying on that narrow bed of his: what the hell was that jackass Stan thinking when he decided to rescue him and send him off to a property owned by Lord Farringdon, the altruistic millionaire who offered up his boarding houses (farmhouses) to hundreds of refugee children, out of the nearly four thousand who had so far reached these shores? Luis had been there for nearly three weeks now, aiding the children as God gave him to understand (though he didn't believe in God); helping by cleaning urinals, doing what he was ordered to do by the English saints of the Basque Children's Committee, from first thing in the morning to very late at night, and all of this just when he was beginning to think his altruistic and philanthropic tendencies (whatever there had been of them) had ended with those Pedagogical Missions which he'd attended tirelessly five or six years ago, yes, back then, when there was no war on the horizon, when everyone (most of his friends, at least) had blindfolds over their eyes, unable to see what was fast approaching, casually discussing classic paintings with timid villagers or even improvising plays at the La Barraca theater with the candid aim of educating the people.

4

He had just turned thirty earlier the same week that he arrived at JFK Airport with the specific intent of staying just long enough for the hatred or rage with which he had abandoned Mexico to begin to wane, or until he was able to bury them a hundred feet underground. When Luis Salerno Insausti arrived in Manhattan and began searching for apartments, newspaper in hand, he nevertheless sensed that the process (the relief) could take him anywhere from three months to twenty years. So far—and this in just the blink of an eye—it had been five: elusive, ephemeral years which passed in a mad rush, like any other occurrence in New York. He was thirty-five years old now and life had spun around as quickly as a colorful top, as is the case with anything that has electrons and is spun resoundingly in the Big Apple, that monstrous toy where time doesn't count … or if it does, it's drained and filtered through sewers and black eddying waters stirred by the agitated footsteps of transient passersby. Time there counts for nothing, Luis now knew from experience, and he was fine with that. In fact, it was even better that way: it was fair and gracious and opportune. In the end, *that's* what he wanted, though he never would have admitted it to himself, even if he had recognized it: it was all about the benevolence of time, time which absolves those who want to settle or forget or alleviate themselves of something mean or nasty or otherwise unpleasant. That's what he'd sought, and that's what he now had. Relief, the ability to forget, a certain (evanescent) internal peace. But how much, really? Just how true was that aforementioned peace, obtained in the bustling solitude of New York? He couldn't be certain, however, at that time, in the passing of that lustrum, that it was first and foremost about abandoning Mexico City, casting his family aside, to cleanse his mouth of the disgusting way things had ended before he left, the difficult, irreconcilable things, the rift that began to emerge just weeks before leaving (finally) the capital … But when, exactly, had it all begun? He couldn't quite remember: all that remained was the dregs of coffee in the gold-rimmed cup. The precise date that the family had become embroiled in conflict couldn't be specified, no matter how hard he tried to recall that distant night. Now he saw in front of him, out there, a slice of the pearl gray moon hanging among the branches of a tree. Or was it a bird? No, it was, of course, the moon, he thought, and lit a second cigarette. Anyway, he said to himself, the grant from the New York Film Academy couldn't have come into his life at a better time, right when he couldn't do it anymore, when he couldn't stand nor *understand* his father, his sister Diana, all those people he knew and thought he loved, when he was inundated by the overwhelming force of differences (the clear, sharp differences) between them, between his father and him, between Diana and him, between the surrounding bourgeois world and him, just another authentic, piece of shit bourgeois man known as Luis Salerno who believed himself (ha ha) to be so un-bourgeois, so un-Babbittish.

Studying cinema, continuing with his love of movies, was little more than a life raft, but it was a life raft in the middle of the raging ocean that his family had turned into overnight. After years of dedication to photography and art films as a mere substitute for what he'd always wanted to be without ever becoming it (a great director), being accepted to NYFA and studying what interested him most in life was like finding a pearl in an oyster in the midst of a stormy sea. He searched for it, he had it (his art, the cinema, New York, the solitude and the hustle), if only deep inside him, but on that night—with that strange email and the empty cup in his hands— he finally caught a glimpse of the fact that all of this was (barely) a façade, the secret alibi, the motive behind it all: leaving Mexico City so that the hatred or anger with which he'd abandoned it (family, too) would slacken or be buried a hundred feet underground in the frozen magma.

5

His friend Jacinto called him on the phone.

"Luis, I have to talk to you."

"So talk to me. What's up?" Luis replied from the other end of the line.

"No, in person. It *has* to be in person."

"It's that important?"

"If it weren't, I'd tell you right now, you moron. We have to do this in person. I don't want you fainting on me."

"Just tell me, you son of a bitch. Don't leave me hanging here," Luis insisted, suddenly intrigued. "What happened? What's wrong? They mess you up? Did someone die?"

"You gotta be kidding me. No, nothing like that. Do I sound upset or pissed off to you?"

"No ... so what is it?"

"I already said I'd tell you in person, damn it. Are you deaf? Can we meet up tomorrow or the day after? You tell me."

"How about today? Right now?" Luis grumbled on the other end of the line.

"I can't do it today. I'm on my way out the door," Jacinto replied, before begrudgingly conceding: "Tomorrow afternoon, if you want. You pick the time. Today's not going to work. Like I said, I'm about to leave the house."

"You're a real bastard, Jacinto."

"Just pick a time. I really have to go."

"Five, or five thirty. Can't do it before that. Having dinner with my parents. I already made plans with them."

"Five o'clock. At my place. Perfect."

"Don't leave me with a fucking cliffhanger ..."

"That's your problem, not mine. Adiós." And with that, Jacinto hung up the phone, leaving an insidious thread of doubt—a poisonous snake—hanging there in the air.

With the gold-rimmed cup still in his hands, Luis Salerno Insau-

sti recalled that (damned) distant night and the phone call from Jacinto; he remembers them because he couldn't fall asleep that night
... but most of all because he couldn't fall asleep the next night, or
the one after that. Three in a row, an insidious, depraved snake. A
new record for insomnia. Hearing Jacinto there in his pied-à-terre
at five o'clock the next day had evidently made things worse: he lost
even more sleep over it and was only able to get it back by swallowing the first little pill of Valium he had ever in his life choked down
into his guts.

After looking once more through his window at the street and
the pearl gray slice of moon, Luis got up from his swivel chair and
went to heat up more water in the little pewter pot that he used
solely for preparing his beloved Turkish coffee. The Spanish espresso
machine sat off in a corner; since Alfredo had given it to him he had
never quite gotten used to it.

6

On April 22nd, 1937, a lovely morning, the old transatlantic ship *Habana* entered the Port of Southampton with 3,800 children on board, accompanied by four nurses, fourteen priests, two doctors, ninety-five teachers and 120 assistants. Two hundred more children continued to make their way to the so called French National Area, before France (as Pontius Pilate had done) cowardly washed their hands of the Spanish dispute. The four thousand youths came from the embattled city of Bilbao, whose government had decided to evacuate them right at the end of the siege, when the Republican defeat had become imminent. Confirmation of asylum, which His Royal Majesty had extended, arrived just in time via the *Royal Oak*, a British battleship sent expressly to the Cantabrian coast to escort these children to their new home. Now, however, there was no other choice but to accept the humiliation of running away from their own country, their own city, their homestead where they lay their heads to rest, without their parents, and all because of their bitter enemies: their own wretched countrymen with crosses on their chests. On April 26th, four days after the children had disembarked, the Luftwaffe destroyed the city of Guernica.

So there they were, that April dawn, hundreds of ragged, dirty, despondent children streaming down the gangplanks, orphans, dozens and dozens of them, helpless, desolate, dazed from the voyage or from war, with no clear idea (or no idea at all) of what they were doing there, or why their mothers hadn't made the trip with them (if they were even still alive). Only the older ones could have had some notion of the place they had arrived to, though probably not, because their first stop upon landing was an improvised refugee camp in the hills of North Stoneham, not far from the port, in Hampshire County. For two or three weeks, those suffering innocents, that hungry and helpless multitude, spent their nights in makeshift tents or even out in the open, if the benevolent weather saw fit, they ate at long wooden tables built specifically for the occasion, and on a big screen they watched movies starring Charlie Chaplin, Buster Keaton, the Marx Brothers, and Harold Lloyd, allowing them, perhaps, for a few short hours to forget about the anguish and uncertainty that hung over them.

All day long, the loudspeakers broadcast instructions in both Spanish and Basque, while the children ran about, playing all over the camp, some with their new soccer balls. Sometimes they fought, others played hide and seek. They all soaked themselves in newfound freedom; however, this was only in appearance, because — unlike at that camp, where order had to be maintained — during the Battle of Bilbao, where they'd come from, those little ones (twelve or thirteen years old) had been, ironically, more free and also more responsible for their freedom, having had to assist family members in the local militia. Side by side, they dug and fortified trenches, loaded rifles, dodged bullets, and buried the bodies of their relatives and neighbors. To a certain extent, before the very recent past began to roil in their minds, these children lived in the present, there in the spring of the English countryside: they were happy in their own precarious way, boisterous and mischievous despite being orphans in exile.

On that June afternoon when the British authorities gathered to announce the fall of Bilbao, a victory for Franco, and therefore the end of any hopes of one day returning to Spain, the older children fainted, collapsing to the ground in anguish while the younger ones bawled inconsolably, a torrent of sorrow which they couldn't quite understand or relate to, but one that swept across the terrified faces of their friends and older siblings, in the broken, dejected posture of the teachers and nurses who had accompanied them in the evacuation and who believed (still believed) that everything, in the end, would work out in a matter of time; a very short time.

Eventually, the two months became two years. When it was all said and done, four hundred children would remain in England forever. The rest were repatriated after the war had ended.

7

The first time he slept with a man was seven or eight months after he'd arrived in New York. It happened at a time when he'd found himself more frustrated and alone than ever, when he could no longer continue to bury all the things that he'd hoped to forget there in the United States, so far from his home, from Diana, from mom, from Marcela, his other sister, the younger one, and—above all— from his father. He was not yet thirty-one years of age.

It was a Chilean guy by the name of Alfredo Tieck, the same as the German novelist whom Alfredo so vainly swore was his grandfather or great-grandfather. The first time Luis saw him, Alfredo's hair cascaded across his forehead in supremely fine, blond waves. Almost immediately, he took a second look. He couldn't help but admire that profile, that light, flowing, waving hair. He wasn't particularly attractive, being neither tall nor strong, but Luis just couldn't tear his eyes away from that face, watching it move back and forth inside the restaurant, seeing it smile at the servers, at the customers sitting in their bastion-like booths, all the bustling life surrounding him as if he, Alfredo, were the nucleus, the flower's corolla: blond hair, lime-green eyes, perfect eyebrows and the thinnest set of lips, which reminded him of those of his mother. Yes, his mother. His hair swung softly across his broad forehead, rising and falling with the slightest movement of his perfectly defined neck, with the pure, graceful hint of an unforeseen gesture. His hair was incredibly straight and not very long: the exact opposite of his own. Salerno Insausti, alone there in the restaurant, not waiting for anyone, couldn't look away. Alfredo, meanwhile, continued smiling for all the world to see ... or so it seemed. The whiteness of his teeth competed with his ermine skin in the dimly lit restaurant. No, Luis later corrected: his teeth competed with the smooth, white, matte finish of his skin.

Subconsciously, as he now recalls, Luis sidled up to the cold mahogany bar where the New Yorkers awaited their tables with a drink and an olive or a handful of peanuts. Suddenly, Alfredo turned towards him and said something in English, as if the two were old friends. He's not a gringo, Luis thought, upon hearing his accent. He hesitated. ¿Hablas español? Sí, por supuesto. And there they were, the two of them standing at the bar, with a pitcher of dark beer filled to the brim. They discussed a few trivialities, each offering the basic details about themselves, about their lives, their countries, their careers, the hustle and bustle of New York City, which Alfredo loved madly, or at least with more passion than did Luis, before finally saying goodbye with a firm handshake until, thirty minutes later, Alfredo's younger sister arrived. The two young men exchanged a few more sentences, and finally they agreed to meet again, after exchanging their respective cell phone numbers.

Alfredo and Luis met the following week at the same restaurant on St. Mark's, but this time without the former's younger sister; the next day they attended a Eugene O'Neill production at NYU where Alfredo was beginning his second semester of his Master's in Business Administration, and two days later they went to a SoHo theater to catch the latest Woody Allen film. They met for coffee three times at the Union Square Barnes & Noble, just across from the New York Film Academy, and—finally—they went out to dinner with Alfredo's sister and her fiancé, another Mexican, three years younger than Luis and Alfredo. But here, at this exact stage of the race—after two weeks of pure dizziness, of attraction hidden behind a veil of heterosexuality—Luis stopped. He stopped short one morning upon leaving the Union Square subway station on his way to his class on directing actors, stood there under the squirrel-filled trees, wondering bewilderedly, were he and Alfredo just two good friends, or was there something more? *What else could they be*, other than a couple of Latin Americans in exile, a couple of companions in a city like a minefield where the solitude can suddenly explode, laying waste to everything? Luis asked himself this question with determination, the morning sun flooding his gaze as he stood there outside the subway station. Was he crazy, imagining things, the kind of queer, sissifying things that might creep into a dirty, impulsive, thirty-something mind? Was there *something* more

20259600

there, or had he been hallucinating it from day one? Nevertheless, and despite the obvious masculinity of his recent friendship, the fact is that Salerno Insausti wasn't entirely sure what, exactly, was going on between them, because at that moment he only *thought* he was feeling *something*, a feeling that he'd never before had for another man, and which, actually, reminded him vaguely of the way he'd occasionally felt about a girl back in Mexico City when he was twenty. He was confused (or trapped in his own, ill-fated sense of solipsism) because absolutely nothing at all had even happened between him and his friend Tieck, or with any other man in his life, for that matter, and yet he was beginning to question and investigate his feelings... because he hadn't so much as held another man's hand, other than his father's or his grandfather's, back when he was still alive.

In other words, until that moment, right there at the subway entrance, he felt—and not much was required in terms of insight—that something not unlike *falling in love* was taking place every time he hung out with Alfredo, every time he contemplated the light, graceful expressions of his face, his eyebrows and the masterfully crafted lines of his neck, his loose, tousled hair, and the thin, fine lips of his mother. Where does the natural attraction between two good "friends" —an intellectual or moral or social sort of attraction—come to an end, and when does it become more of a desire, an aesthetic and physical sort of magnetism? Clearly, when appropriate, the two things (the two attractions) were equal, neither greater than the other, neither above the other, because the fact was that Luis was just as engrossed in debating Wall Street finance over coffee with Alfredo as he was entranced by the gentle curvature of his lips and his long, veined hands.

When it came to women, they spoke one time and one time only, in a single, flaming burst. Strange, too: the thorny issue was just as quickly set aside. They laughed awkwardly, looked around, avoiding eye contact, and the subject was never brought up again.

8

"Okay now, tell me what it's all about."

Luis had Jacinto (dark, diminutive, and bespectacled) in front of him; between them sat the enormous, second-hand writing desk which, for some strange reason, occupied the center of his friend's luxurious studio apartment (located near the Miguel Alemán freeway, and which Jacinto referred to as a pied-à-terre, though in reality it was little more than a wide living room, bathroom, and kitchenette with a refrigerator). The rest of the space was taken up by books loosely stacked against the walls, in each and every corner, books wherever the eye could see, except for two large windows through which a particular radiance of unfiltered light was currently pouring.

"Okay Luis, look, first of all, let me say two things. First, I'm not sure whether you already know what I'm about to tell you. I mean, I don't know if you told me once and I forgot about it, or even if you knew all along and just never mentioned it ..." Here Jacinto paused for a second, if only to confirm the look of total shock in his best friend's eyes. "If that's the case, if it was *your* secret, well, I want you to know that I know too. My mother told me, okay? And you deserve to know that I know."

"I have no idea what you're talking about," Luis complained hotly, growing ever more uncomfortable in his seat at the enormous table in the center of the room. "Can you please get to the point, Jacinto? It's your fucking fault I didn't sleep a wink last night, so now's the time for you to start clearing things up."

"My fault?"

"Of course it's your fault, you son of a bitch, because you left me hanging after that phone call ... So start talking already! You're pissing me off with all this cloak-and-dagger stuff."

"I told you I had two things to lay out first. I've given you the first one, right?"

FRANKLIN COUNTY LIBRARY
906 NORTH MAIN STREET
LOUISBURG, NC 27549
BRANCHES IN BUNN,
FRANKLINTON, & YOUNGSVILLE

"Yes, a string of words that made no sense, of course, but fine …" Luis drummed his fingers impatiently on the desk, like a terminally ill patient awaiting a grim diagnosis from his doctor. And to make matters worse, he'd left his cigarettes in the car. "So what the fuck is the second one?"

"That I really don't know if I *should* be telling you this—because you might not know—and for the plain and simple reason that I don't want this to upset you."

"Upset me?"

"Yes, I don't want this to hurt you, if you truly *don't* already know. It's messed up, I know, but …"

"I know, I know, you're a homo, Jacinto. That's it. You're gay. Is that what this is all about? You're gay and you were too ashamed to tell me."

"No, you moron …" Jacinto stood up from his seat and groaned in frustration, annoyed that the revelation of such a mystery had started off as such a disaster on that very uncomfortable evening. "I'm not a fucking fag. The only fag here is you. You're the one who hasn't had a girlfriend in forever. It's been over two years since you even fucked someone. If anyone here is gay, it's you, Luis! Ha!"

They both laughed.

Now (far away from all that, all alone in his Manhattan apartment) as Salerno Insausti recalled Jacinto's acute outburst that memorable evening, he couldn't help but smile weakly at the confirmation that his friend was, after all, right: it was him, Luis, who was the fag. At least now he was. Back then, when that strange encounter with Jacinto took place, some five and a half years before, he couldn't even imagine that just twelve months later he *would indeed* find the courage to sleep with whomever he wanted and admit that he wasn't *necessarily* attracted to women. That gutsy bit of bravery showed through in the end, yes, and *the one* would appear—as he now knew—in the slender form of Alfredo Tieck, the exquisite blond Chilean with the surname of a German novelist, and the grandson or great-grandson of a romance writer to boot.

"So?" Luis pressed on through the grainy afternoon light. "Are you going to tell me or not?"

Jacinto took a deep breath before finally letting it all out:

"You have a sister."

"What are you saying?"

"I'm saying that besides the two sisters you know, you have a half sister."

"I have another sister besides Diana and Marcela?"

"Yes, you heard me right."

"Who told you this?"

"My mom did. I already told you that."

"And how the fuck would your mom know that, Jacinto? How could she be so sure? Does she know her?"

"No, she doesn't."

"So?"

"It's a little complicated, Luis."

"I don't care if it's complicated. You're gonna tell me what you know right now. We've got all the time in the world, because I'm not leaving this spot until you tell me everything."

"So you had no idea about any of this?"

"Of course not ..." He cut in, stopping his friend short. "Now you tell me, Jacinto: how would your mom know anything about this?"

"I'm not quite sure ... I think my mom has a friend at the club where she plays tennis on the weekends ..."

"Okay ... and?"

"They wanted to relax in the sauna after playing a couple of sets ..."

"What else?" Impatient, almost violent, Luis was tapping his fingers faster and faster on his friend's table. All that was missing was the cigarette.

"So they started chatting in the sauna."

"Skip past the part about the sauna, please."

"Anyway, it turns out that the woman knows another woman who apparently is none other than your sister's mom. Your *half* sister, Luis, since she—your new sister—is only related to you through your father."

"I know how it works, asshole." Luis stopped fidgeting with his fingers and immediately asked, "So how did your mom and this other woman figure all that out?"

"Because she, your half sister, has the same last name as you. Salerno. Salerno Yanguas, I think."

"And what the hell is her first name, if you don't mind me asking?"

"Amparo."

"Amparo?"

"That's what the other woman told my mom in the sauna ... Anyway, as you might have guessed, it all boiled down to the last name, Salerno, which I think we can agree is not very common." At this point, Jacinto nervously crossed and uncrossed his legs and adjusted his glasses. "When she heard that name, my mother loudly exclaimed that her son's best friend—that's you—is also named Salerno. Luis Salerno."

"You're right, there aren't too many people with that last name," Luis added, at once mortified and joyful to hear the extremely unexpected news that he had a half sister.

"And that's not all ... it sounds like your sister Amparo is convinced that her father is your father."

"She's sure?" Luis's eyes were as wide as dinner plates.

"It seems so."

"So why didn't I know about this?"

"I have no idea," Jacinto replied on that distant afternoon, shortly after five o'clock. "But the fact is, Luis, that I wasn't sure whether you already knew about all this and maybe even mentioned it to me once, or whether it was a secret you couldn't entrust to me or anyone else for that matter ... one of those family secrets that everyone's got, you know?"

"I don't know anything about anything. Nobody's spoken so much as a word about this to me in my entire life."

"I can see."

"All that being said, how did the connection come up? You haven't explained that part."

"Apparently, it's a well-known thing. Very well known."

"Well known? What does that mean?"

"It means that my mother's friend—who knows Amparo's mother—spoke about it quite naturally, as if it were just common knowledge. Like there was no mystery or secrecy surrounding it. Understand? When she heard the last name there in the sauna, my mom just blurted out your name, and the other woman replied, 'Yeah, Luis, Amparo's father,' clearly thinking they were talking about your father, not you."

"And your mom corrected this lady?"

"Of course. She said, 'My son's friend is Luis Salerno Insausti. The son, not the father.'"

"So from what you're telling me ... on her side of the family—Amparo's side—*they* all know about this?"

"It would seem so."

"But on my side of the family, nobody does."

"..."

"Am I wrong?"

"..."

Luis, though, was able to answer that question for himself, without needing any confirmation from Jacinto. He paused for a moment. Closed his eyes, as if to reflect.

"Does my father know?"

"How would I know that?"

"He must know ... he has to ..."

"..."

"You can't be a father just like that, without knowing it."

"Actually, Luis, you can't be a *mother* without knowing about it. When it comes to being a father, it's a bit more complicated. Maybe you know and maybe you don't. Maybe she told you, and maybe she didn't. Maybe you don't even want to know. But please, you can just take it for what it's worth."

Luis hadn't even heard him. He had already stood up from his chair, lost halfway between bewilderment and anxiousness, between grumpy and happy at having heard the news, invaded by an indescribable emotion: a mix of surprise, disbelief, credulity, joy, disappointment, helplessness, and curiosity to meet this sister of his, this Amparo Salerno Yanguas.

A short while later, in the fading afternoon light, still pensive, still ceaselessly pacing up and down between the stacks of books lining the walls of Jacinto's sparse living room, he suddenly asked:

"Can you get my half sister's phone number?" Immediately, he added, "I'm begging you. Ask your mom."

"I knew it. I knew it. I saw this coming."

"You knew what, Jacinto?"

"I knew you were gonna ask me that, and that everything was gonna get even more complicated. Damn it. I should have just listened to my mom and kept my trap shut."

"What's so fucking complicated about a phone number, Jacinto?"

"Be serious for a minute, Luis. You know full well what I'm saying. The complicated stuff has yet to come. Listen to me ... you have no idea. You have no idea how this is all going to turn out." And boy was Jacinto right, Luis thought, as he dumped two spoonsful of coffee into the boiling water before switching off the tiny stove a moment later. Then he looked out the window at the gray slice of moon hanging there among the Manhattan trees.

"What are you talking about?"

"Something you have no idea about, asshole. Something you've spent your entire life completely oblivious to, and now I come along like an idiot and tell you all about it, when probably—clearly—it would have been better if you'd never known. Mea culpa."

"You wouldn't have told me if you weren't my best friend, Jacinto. You know that."

"Yeah, I know."

"I would have done the same. I would have told you too." Luis tossed a heaping spoonful of sugar into the little pewter pot, despite the fact that he preferred it bitter, black. Now he had to let the coffee sit, settle, like the soul, like the four humors.

Suddenly the waxing Manhattan moon had lost the pearly gray color of a giant oyster, transforming instead into a sterner sepia, or yellow.

9

Not being brutally murdered like Federico, or not being imprisoned in late '37 or early '38, was (he had to admit) thanks to the one man who annoyed him more than any other man on Earth, and with whom he'd also had a very brief romantic relationship, though it never (ever) gave him pleasure: the poet and translator of a number of his own poems, the eccentric and mendacious Stanley Richardson. Such cruel irony! Here he was, right now, in England, on this damn island, safe from retaliatory bullets fired by the surging Fascists, more depressed and impotent than he had ever felt throughout his existence, all because of (or thanks to) being more deplorable than the man with whom he'd locked himself in a relationship. He should be eternally grateful to this man, it's true, but the fact is that he just couldn't bring himself to behave well enough to thank him for everything he should be thankful for. Instead, one night, after living with Stan in his luxurious London flat for two weeks, he said:

"I can't stay here with you anymore. I'm sorry, but I really can't. I appreciate everything that you've done for me, Stan, for bringing me here and putting me up for a few days, but I just can't live with you."

"But what happened?" the young poet with the nearly transparent blue eyes asked, stunned.

"I don't feel quite right here. You've been more than kind, but I have to go."

"You *have* to go? I don't understand . . ."

"I *need* to go. I *want* to go," Cernuda replied categorically, raising the tone of his voice just a bit.

"But Luis, where will you go?"

"To Spain."

"Are you insane?"

"Yes, I suppose I must be."

"Spain? So you can get yourself killed? They'll crucify you if you go back there. You know that."

"There's nothing left to talk about. I'm going, Stanley. I just can't stand it anymore." He had wanted to say, I can't stand *you* anymore, but he restrained himself. It was enough. He had already been too eloquent.

All but discerning the intent behind Luis's words (the words which Cernuda didn't dare to speak, despite always being quite frank with the world), Richardson asked him, with tears welling up in his eyes:

"But what have I done, Luis? Was it something I said? Something I missed? Tell me how I let you down?"

"Nothing, nothing at all. It's not something you said, not something you did."

"So?"

"So … that's it. I'm leaving."

After a few seconds of silence, a few tricky and difficult seconds, a devastated look in his tearful eyes, Richardson began to blubber:

"Fine. If that's what you want—if you don't love me anymore—I can't keep you locked up in here. All I ask is that you don't go back to Spain. It's pure madness, Luis. Being able to leave was nothing short of a miracle. Don't go back. I'm begging you. If you don't want to do it for me or for yourself, do it for the memory of Federico, may he rest in peace, for our friendship, for the wonderful time we all spent in Madrid, remember? When I met you, and we were all friends: Vicente, Morla, Manolo, Concha, Federico, Alberti and his wife, you, me. Do it for Federico. And if you want, you can talk with my godmother. She knows everyone. With her contacts, we can find something for you, something decent, something soon, I promise you. You could teach at any school."

"Stan, that's what you said when I got here, when you brought me here to England, remember? You promised me well-paying lectures and readings, but none of that came about. I can't live off your scraps … I need to earn a living somehow. I don't even have enough money to buy a movie ticket."

"You'll pay me back one day, but don't go back to Spain. No matter how much you want to, Luis, don't do it now. If you don't want to live here with me, I won't blame you. It hurts my soul, but that's fine. I just want you to be safe, and going back to Spain, the way things are, is utter nonsense. You know that better than anyone."

"I'll give you a week," Luis replied. "After that, I'm moving on, Stan."

And here he was, six weeks later, with the Vullioni family. Stanley had fulfilled his promise: on the eighth day, Luis was able to move out of the apartment and move in with friends of the Richardsons in Oxfordshire. He'd done what he had to do; however, he wasn't sure whether he'd ended up worse off than before, with that situation in Stan's London flat. Although (on the bright side) nothing in this world could actually be worse than continuing on with that awful lover who just didn't seem to understand that what they'd had was in the *past*, than he no longer loved him and would never love him again, no matter how badly he willed it to be otherwise. The summers of '34 and '35 in Madrid were forgotten things. The problem, of course, was that for Richardson *those things* were very much still alive, my God. And the most unpleasant part of this entire mess was that—if there was something that cut to the very core of his being, something that truly infuriated him—it was the sin of being ungrateful. That was something he couldn't take. He couldn't stand ingrates and ungratefulness, and yet here he was, behaving like the most unappreciative one of all. He couldn't believe it was a part of him, of his nature, of his complicated inner self . . . however complicated it might have been, and however poorly Richardson was able to read into it. He, Luis, was the most ungrateful man on Earth, and it was all because of Stanley: he was an obstinate one, and Luis despised him intimately because of it. Because of that stubborn sense of generosity, which had led the Englishman to save him, Luis was horrified at himself, and that, paradoxically, led him to hate the young poet even more, despite the fact that he had opened his home to him, nourished and sustained him, and pulled him from the clutches of his own native land with clever words and delicate deceptions. Going to England was *supposedly* about attending a series of conferences, which Stan had apparently organized at a number of colleges and universities, and for which he would be earning a generous speaker's fee (and he certainly needed the money to keep on rolling along!). Immediately after delivering these lectures, Luis stated in his last letter before leaving Spain via Paris, he would be returning to Madrid, to his home (although the fact was that the house was never actually his; he'd taken it over after his mother had died over ten years before). The conferences at Oxford and Cambridge were, in the end, a total fiasco, more of a swindle, really, for the remuneration was next to nothing at all. It was all a hoax, a lure Richardson had used to reel him in, to get him back, keep him sheltered there in his house and recreate the love they had once made four years earlier, recently returned from Pedagogical Missions in Málaga and Toledo. One giant ruse to save his life and get him out of that absurd war. Was it pure egoism? Luis would ask himself at night (and that particular night) as he lay there in the narrow bed in the spare room of the Vullioni home. Or was it pure altruism and selfless generosity that Stan had shown? These questions notwithstanding, Luis was sharp enough not to fall into easy Manichaeisms. He knew that nothing was the color with which it is painted; nothing is black or white, nor is it good or bad, Fascist or Republican. He understood better than ever that all men are the same in one particular way: they're all just a bunch of downright bastards. Some believe that what they're doing is righteous, while those doing the opposite believe the exact same thing. But in either case, men do what they do out of pure blindness or simply to fuck each other over, because you don't think the way I do, because you don't like and respect what I do, because you don't want what my people and I do, because you're not like me. Therefore I kill you, therefore I annihilate you, or rather, as Stanley did, therefore I save you and deceive you, therefore I pluck you out of your country and bring you into my own, I tie you up in my chair, trapping you in my home, sleeping in my bed, eating at my table. And there you have it. That is why Stanley's generosity aggravated him so much. Because he knew that what lay behind that façade was nothing more than the most primal sense of egoism: satisfying his own whims and desires, feeding the sovereign pleasures of his body, and the rush of that momentum satisfied him, that much was clear, lying next to him in bed, between the sheets, with the pretext of war. When he tried to explain all this to Rafael Martínez Nadal, whom he saw from time to time at his Queen's Court flat, right near the old Kensington Palace, he either couldn't quite find the right words, or he didn't know how to explain himself. This was all quite difficult, a ball of yarn that would take centuries to unravel without being equivocal, ambiguous, or reductionistic. He didn't know how to begin or how to examine those fine threads which—whether he wanted it or not—had tied him into this relationship with a man who had put a roof over his head, supporting him, caring for him, protecting him from certain death in Spain. On the one hand, it was so hard to not be grateful to that mellifluous poet with the oval-shaped head, the obstinate translator of his own verses, but on the other hand, it was so easy to detest, to pillory, to mock that young, snobbish piece of trash. With each passing day, his hatred grew towards his affable and pompous manners, the brazen manner in which he attracted attention at the Café Royal, his ridiculous eccentricity and attire, and even the affected considerations he had for him. All of this was all but inexplicable to good old Rafael, who sat there, listening, with a cup of tea in hand, while his sister Lola and his delightful mother sat in the dining room knitting or reading the latest novel by Vicente Blasco Ibáñez, who was quite in fashion at the time.

10

Alfredo's sister Guillermina Tieck was there visiting with her Mexican fiancé, Manuel, who had received a Ph.D. in economics from Cornell, and came to New York specifically to be with Guille. Alfredo set up the dinner at a little Greek restaurant, Pylos, in the heart of the East Village, a place he'd been wanting to visit with Luis ever since ever since the topic of gastronomy had been raised at Barnes & Noble the first or second time they met there to leaf through books on the inexistence of God and the phenomenon of religion. However, the night of the dinner at Pylos (the seventh or eighth time they'd seen one another) was not only memorable but also revelatory for Salerno, in more ways than one. Before clarifying the first revelation, it must be said that second one was obvious, radical, and extremely concrete: after saying goodnight to Alfredo's sister and to Manuel, Luis would—for the first time—sleep with a man. The second revelation came up during the midst of that sumptuous dinner, which included three bottles of Greek wine, eggplant moussaka, onion and veal dolmathes, garlic and crab meat kavouro keftedes, tzatziki sauce with cucumbers and mint, roasted red peppers filled with spicy feta cheese, pear and arugula salad, and some extraordinary savory phyllo pastries filled with Cretan honey-braised lamb and spinach rice pilaf.

How did that whole night begin? Luis didn't know, and Alfredo couldn't remember. Who'd started that Byzantine discussion? Neither of them could answer that question either, when they talked about it the next morning there in Alfredo's bed, languid and incredulous as to what had just happened, their bodies warmly entwined in the morning sun. All that notwithstanding, the only certainty was that suddenly, amidst the Greek wine, the aroma of the candle in the middle of the table, and the clay pots hanging all throughout the restaurant like some extravagant shrine honoring the name of Pylos, they heard the twenty-two-year-old Guille ask her young fiancé:

"Manuel, what would you do if, say, we've been married for seven years, have two little kids who are three and five, we love them and we love each other as much as we do here today, everything's going great between us … and then suddenly, somehow, you find out that you have another child?"

"Another child?" the young Mexican exclaimed.

"I'm asking you because something similar happened to Vivi, the sister of a very good friend of mine from Santiago …"

"Vivi?" Alfredo asked.

"No, one of Vivi's friends. You don't know her, Alfredo," Guille corrected herself before turning back to her fiancé to repeat, mercilessly, the question again: "So what would you do, Manuel?"

"So what you're saying is that it's my kid but not *yours*? Not *ours*?" Poor Manuel's ears were all plugged up; either that, or he was desperately searching for more time to think about how to respond to this disgraceful question posed by his Chilean fiancée.

"Yes, exactly," Guille drove the point home, brandishing her glass like a viniferous sword.

"What kind of a question is that!" Alfredo interjected, attempting to head off an argument between his sister and his friend Luis's poor fellow countryman.

"It could happen to anyone, Alfredo," his sister replied without once turning her stern look away from her fiancé, who was sitting immediately to her left and who looked smaller by the moment in the face of such a surprising attack. "Even you, big bro. How would you know? You could have a son or daughter in Viña del Mar or Santiago and you have no idea. Just think about it!"

"Yeah, that would be a bitter pill to swallow, wouldn't it?" Luis thought to ask, turning to face Alfredo, who was sitting to his right.

"It'd be bad. It'd be really bad," he replied, but then quickly flipped the conversation back. "But I think this is about Manuel, not me. The question is directed at you, mano …"

Alfredo used the word "mano" the way Mexicans do: short for "manito" or "hermanito." Luis wasn't sure whether he'd learned that phrase from him or from someone else before that, but he began to feel—in spite of himself—just a slight hint of jealousy that quickly faded when he heard Guillermina go back to asking Manuel that same, convoluted question, to which he responded:

"So how do I find out about it, Guille?"

"What are you, a detective? That's totally beside the point," she replied angrily. "The baby's mother calls you up and let's you know. Or maybe, it's a mutual friend. Or she doesn't want the kid. Whatever, it's not important, Manuel. The fact of the matter is that it's yours and you have to start taking care of it today."

"Today?"

"Don't be stupid!" she shouted. "*Today* means after we've married for seven years, remember? That's the context."

"Clearly."

"So today, Manuel, you and I have two daughters together," she insisted harshly.

"Did this all happen before or after the two of us got married, Guillermina?" Luis asked, trapped in this discussion though still curious, almost as if it were describing his own life.

"Of course it would have been before! Otherwise, we wouldn't even be having this conversation," the young, emboldened, and proudly feminist Chilean woman replied. "What do you take me for, some idiot who lets herself be outwitted by her own fiancé?"

"That's not what he said! Just calm down," Alfredo interjected, defending Luis. "He was only asking so he could see the bigger picture …"

"I apologize," she said, her eyes fixed on the tablecloth. "It must be the wine."

"You almost never drink, little sis."

"Everyone take it easy!" Salerno Insausti said, lifting his glass, determined from that moment to keep his mouth shut: he wasn't about to ruin those dolmathes and the lamb-stuffed phyllo pastries all because of that spoiled girl who was making dinner quite dicey for his poor fellow countryman, the Cornell economist.

"And so?" Alfredo pressed, turning to face Manuel.

"Well, I'd talk with you, Guille, and we'd see if we could raise the child together, bring it home, educate it, make it our own, love it … what do I know!"

"A new brother or sister for our two girls?" she replied with some hesitancy.

"Well, that's what it would be, right? Yeah, they're siblings." Manuel paused nervously, not quite sure whether he'd responded correctly. "Half siblings. That's what they'd be, Guille."

"Are you insane?" fumed the young Chilean woman.

"But it's my kid … isn't that what you just said? No way I'm leaving my child out on the streets, or in a foster home. I'm not going to turn my back on him after we've only barely met."

"Well, that would be your problem, not mine," Guille said, blinded by her fiancé's response. "You would have to choose, Manuel. Either that child or us: your daughters and me."

"Forgive me for cutting in," Alfredo said quickly, "but you're not offering much in the way of options, Guille. Not to mention the fact that—if you're married, if you're a loving couple—then it's your problem too, not just his. It sounds like Manuel would be willing to talk about it, make a case for it, and come to a fair and acceptable solution … He can't leave his own child on the streets, just like that … Again, the problem would be for the both of you, and it would be up to the both of you to find a resolution, Guille. That is, of course, if you love him."

"No, no way, Alfredo. You're all wrong on this one."

"How?" he insisted, evidently upset with his younger sister. "Tell me."

"Because the problem started before Manuel met me. Therefore, in no way, shape, or form is it our problem. That's his problem. It's his kid; not mine. Understand?"

"Stop right there!" Luis erupted, furious enough at what he'd just heard to break his own vow of silence. "So according to you, Guille, having a child is a problem."

"That's not what I meant," the young, suddenly repentant Chilean woman said, caught in Luis's argument.

"But that's what you said … and that means it's what you were thinking, too, Guille," Salerno Insausti finished angrily.

"But I don't get it, sis …" Alfredo jumped in, trying unsuccessfully to come to her aid. "If it happened before you two met, it's wrong, and if it happened during your marriage, it would also be wrong. There's no way out with you. You have to open up, you have to be willing to communicate, to reconcile things with your husband."

"Exactly," Guille said, with a touch of stubborn arrogance. "Manuel should tell me, right now, if he has another child with some little Mexican girl, don't you think? He should tell me now and not later, when it's already too late, when we're already a fully formed and functioning family."

"But what if I don't know? I really have no idea," Manuel confessed, his voice wavering. "I guess I don't think I do. If I knew I did, I would tell you, Guille. You know that."

"You think you don't or you're sure you don't, Manuel? Those are two very different things."

"No one can be sure of anything," cautioned Guillermina's brother, "except for the women who give birth to the children … and not even then, you know, because what if two babies were switched in the nursery and nobody ever realized it. You just said it yourself: what if it's me, your brother, who has a child in Chile, and I have no idea about it. You see? You're contradicting yourself. You just can't be reasoned with."

"Enough already," Luis intervened, hoping to bring a bit of order back to the situation while chewing on a bit of feta cheese. "Let's put this to rest now, shall we?"

"No, Luis …" Manuel grabbed his arm, clearly incensed and finally willing to answer a question that he never in his life had wanted to hear and which was nevertheless put forward by his fiancée. "If I have to choose — if that's what you're forcing me to do — then I would choose my unknown child over my two daughters and you. That's it. Am I making myself clear? You hear me, Luis? You hear me, Alfredo? Now everyone knows."

Silence echoed across the table. No one picked up a glass nor set one down on the stained tablecloth; not so much as a finger twitched. The only movement was the curling of the wick in the candle that sat between them and the smoke slowly spreading across the table like a plague or some floating, indigo ghost.

"But why?" Luis asked hesitantly, more to break the icy silence than anything.

"I guess because my daughters have had me for four or five years or whatever it was. But this child hasn't had a father since the day he was born. And I'm saying, I'm asking, how would it be the child's fault if I were the father and didn't know it, if his mother never told me about him, that he'd had to grow up without a dad? For me, that would be the only ethical way to act ... Of course, that's with the understanding that I know what I've got. If I don't know anything, I can't do anything. It's that simple."

"Ethical? That's the only ethical way to act?" Guillermina said, groaning and moaning with either anger or pain: was it the alcohol, or was it all much more serious than any of them (Alfredo, Luis, and Manuel) could have imagined at the time?

"Look, Luis," Manuel said, addressing Salerno specifically, as if there were no one else at the table. "I'm not saying that's the decision I'd feel happiest about, but I think, deep down, that it would be the fair choice, the right choice, the consistent choice, especially since my wife isn't giving me any other alternatives," Manuel insisted, truly upset with this entirely stupid conversation. "Should we always do what we want to do, or what we *have* to do, what we know we *should* do in life?"

"Honestly, I'm not quite sure," Alfredo said, and who knows whether he was actually considering the question or just simply trying to settle the difficult situation once and for all. "I think that fundamentally our actions are based on egoism, not altruism, Manuel. Whether we know it or not, whether we like it or not, what we do and don't do is out of self-interest, pure and simple. Not because of some sense of responsibility or fairness, and not necessarily because it's right."

"Self-interest, perhaps, but also out of consistency, Alfredo. Out of the need to be consistent with ourselves," Luis chimed in, supporting Manuel. "That's what Manuel said: consistent. And you're ethical when you're being consistent ..."

"Yes, Luis," Alfredo replied, "but also because *doing so* feels immensely gratifying. Clearly, Manuel would feel happy about this decision: the one that, for him, is the right one, the correct one. Essentially, my point is this: what we call ethics, 'our ethics,' doesn't lie deep within us, but rather in our most pure and intimate sense of joy. In other words, it's the value we place on our own happiness. And of course, everyone understands happiness differently. That's why, if the selfishness of wanting to be happy wasn't the most valuable of all values—the supreme value—then we wouldn't ever be ethical."

"Says who?" Guille asked, astonished.

"Nietzsche," Alfredo replied. "And four hundred years before him, Spinoza said it too. Even Aristotle rattled on about it ... though he never got into the issue of egoism, which inevitably involves the issue of happiness, something he called Eudemian."

Luis didn't know what to say. He was perplexed: Alfredo was right, but Manuel was right as well. Or that's what he thought at the time. And all that notwithstanding, Guillermina—in her inextricable femininity—was also right. At least in her own way. All three of them were right, but all for quite different reasons ... unequal, and complicated, whichever way you looked at it. The fact that he, himself, or Manuel or Alfredo, for example, didn't understand Guillermina or know how to assess her intricate perspective didn't mean that Guillermina was wrong. It just so happened that she didn't think the same as her boyfriend. She simply didn't feel the way Manuel or the other two did. For Guillermina, her daughters were here daughters and that was that. The other child was nobody, absolutely nobody: if anything, it was her husband's child or her soon-to-be husband's child, but that was accidental, and—ultimately—it hadn't been her accident; it was nothing more than circumstantial, and therefore, in the end, it wasn't her concern.

But then, what about the paternity? Luis wondered to himself as he tipped back his glass and listened to the comments flying back and forth across the busy table. An accident? Nothing more than circumstance? A sperm cell crashing into an egg in sidereal space? When does paternity begin, when does it end? Maybe it's the day Manuel (hypothetically) fathers the child, or is it the day when, hypothetically, Manuel *learns that he has this child,* seven or eight years later? When, exactly, does paternity begin? And if he doesn't find out about it until much, much later, could he possibly *remedy* the situation? But even if he could, how would he go about it? Does he feel any sense of being a daddy-come-lately? And what age—at what point in the child's life—is it too late to become a father? Thirty? Twenty? Ten? Five? One month? What the hell *is* a father, even? Are there a number of different types, all of them valid, or is there but one true form surrounded by substitutes, mere simulacra of an objective, universal fatherhood? As he mulled all this over in his mind, Luis twirled his glass without really paying attention to his three fellow diners. Is a father simply someone who *has* a child, or is it someone who *knows* he has a child? These are two very distinct questions. Could I have a child, could I *be a father* without ever knowing it and end up dying completely unawares, having lived my whole life in a state of utter ignorance? But what if you find out one day (sooner or later) ... does that automatically transform you into a dad? Even if you're not a father in the legal or moral sense, and—if anything—only biologically?

Luis felt the urge to light a cigarette. Maybe you don't become a dad for any of those reasons, he decided. Maybe you just *are,* you're a father when you take it on? Yes, yes, that was it ... But if that's the case, Luis paused to think again, then what does taking it on really mean? How do you do it? What's the standard? Is it piece by piece, bit by bit, day by day, by comparing percentages? Do you need one hundred percent, or is fifty percent more than enough? How the hell do you assume the role of father? Does it have something to do with what Manuel calls responsibility, fairness, ethics? Or do you have to be a real egoist to be a good dad, a great dad, if—as Alfredo believes—we do everything we do out of pure pleasure and gratification, because it makes us happy, whether we're aware of it or we're not, whether we know Nietzsche and Spinoza or we don't? Can you take on something as vague and encompassing as father-hood—something you can't shake off, something grafted into you like an organ, or even more so than an organ, considering that, in the end, you can detach yourself from a kidney but never from a child? He was beginning to feel dizzy ... How can I be a father if I don't know anything, if nobody has spoken so much as a word to me, if I have no idea that I have a child? Perhaps you only assume the role on the day the child (your child?) calls you "Dada," and not a day before? Is that the day when everything is set in motion? Or does it happen when you choose to become one, the day on which you choose, with absolute freedom, to take charge of your own pa-ternity? How would that work? Who has the final word on this? You or the child?

He excused himself and stepped out for a breath of air. In fact, he really needed a cigarette.

11

He spooned some sugar into his Turkish coffee and took a sip. He almost never added sugar to his coffee, and this time, he regretted it. He set the gold-rimmed cup off to one side of the table. Then he wrote:

Dear sis,

Thank you for the email, and forgive me for taking so long to respond. I haven't done much, other than edit a short film by my Spanish friend, whom I've told you about, and now I'm preparing to shoot a little piece of my own in Central Park with a group of amateur actors. Still, you know, the editing, as opposed to filming, is always a pain: it is, perhaps, the most important part of the story and nobody who watches the film will ever understand the sleepless nights that you spend giving coherence to the narrative, creating the marvelous illusion of a *continuum*, even when the story is fragmentary, as with *Memento* or *21 Grams*. Editors, you know, are some of the most saintly men in films, and they barely even appear in the credits. That's why I want to be a director, ha ha, that's why I came to New York. But you still have to get through the editing and a thousand other things I don't like to do, and I'd better stop here before I bore you. As soon as I get this new short filmed, I'll let you know how it went.

As you said, it's been five years since we've seen each other, Marcela, five years since I left Mexico without so much as an idea of when I might set foot there again. Time has flown right by us, hasn't it? I don't know what we would have done—what I would have done—without the fucking internet, or the blessing of your emails: long-distance phone calls would be impossible to pay. I confess that it hurts a bit that you haven't been able to visit me here in New York during these past five years; neither you nor Augusto have taken any time off, not even a weekend, and you both deserve it. It's really too bad. I would have loved to welcome you here and to stroll around SoHo, Fifth Avenue, Chinatown, and Broadway; visit the MoMA, Central Park, and Rockefeller Center; and take you to dinner at Pylos, the best Greek restaurant in New York. You can't imagine what this city is like! At all hours of the day or night there is commotion, chaos, utter confusion, and crowds of people that come and go without rhyme or reason! That part, I suppose, makes everything more bearable, more breathable, despite the fact that — as you know — I'm struggling to find and preserve my solitude, my space.

How are the children? Growing? Are they tough to handle? I can't believe I only know little José through the photos you send me; I think he looks like me when I was little, no? When I left Mexico City, you were pregnant, so he must be a little over four years old now, and Fernando would be eight … It's interesting, I've never met José, and yet I love him just as much as I love you and Fernando. I love them both as if they were my own sons, and I've never even hugged José. And that, just so you know, is something for which I will never forgive myself. That's the unpleasant part of my exile in New York: connections are lost, memories are blurred, and on top of all that, you fantasize about the lives of others, the ones who stayed behind, you wonder about your loved ones, about what they might or might not do this weekend: a birthday, someone's wedding, so-and-so's wild party. So once you've chosen the life of an expat, you should plant yourself solidly in your chosen place and live a life there, create one, surround yourself with people, with the world, build bonds, build a routine.

Well, this email is also to let you know that lately I've been hounded by an obsessive idea: returning to Mexico. Just a quick trip, of course, and just to see my nephews; actually, to see Fernando again, and to see José for the first time. If I'm not mistaken, I might have hinted at my desire to return in a previous message. It's a pretty strange pilgrimage, I know. For one, having let so many years slip by, and now, all of a sudden, feeling the urge to see you and the boys. But what can you do? That's life, isn't it? I guess you could say I'm crazy.

You know, Marcela, that despite it all there are a number of fundamental things preventing me from coming home for good, including Dad, whom I haven't seen or even spoken to since I left (and perhaps before then), and also Diana, whom I haven't been able to forgive nor understand. I haven't corresponded with either of them, and we certainly haven't spoken on the phone, you know? I don't know what it would be like seeing her and Dad again. Sometimes I imagine myself sitting face to face with both of them, having coffee there at your house, in no man's land, and even the taste of the coffee makes me bitter, can you believe it? The last I heard from Diana was an email she sent to wish me a happy birthday last year, but I didn't reply. I wouldn't, or couldn't. I can't remember either way. I'm sure she's told you, and both of them will say that I'm just being resentful, but that's not it, I swear to you that isn't it. It was all just too much for me. I guess it has to do with my confusion, my complete lack of understanding of how our father (an upright, honorable man) treated Amparo, his daughter, our half sister, no matter what he says, whatever excuse he gives. I just don't get it, nor do I understand what Diana and Dad did behind our backs.

Well then, I don't want to be a pain, Marcela. I just needed to write these lines to you (I guess I'm feeling very alone, for a change, which is how I like it, or so I say, ha ha). To tell you that I'm doing well for the most part (as well as could be expected) and that sooner or later I'll realize whether I really want to go back to Mexico or whether that's just a passing fancy and what's really moving me is something much more profound and, to a certain extent, uncertain. But I do know one thing right now: I really do want to see my nephews, who, as you know, are like my own sons, the sons I never had.

Kisses to you and the kids, and another big kiss for Mom when you see her, and hugs for Augusto.

Your brother,
Luis

12

Luis was crossing the threshold of adolescence and was about to leave the house where he had been born and lived until then, for another on the outskirts of the city. It was a mild and luminous March afternoon, suffused with the look and feel and smell of early spring in that nearly uninhabited landscape.

He was standing in the empty room that was to be his in the new house, and through the open window the breeze was blowing the pure young aroma of the countryside, brightening the flame of the green and golden light, increasing the power of the afternoon. Leaning against the window frame, nostalgic without knowing what for, he gazed at the landscape a long while.

In a kind of intuition more than perception, for the first time in his life he sensed the beauty of everything his eyes beheld. And with the vision of that hidden beauty a feeling of solitude he'd never known before slipped into him like something stabbing his soul.

The weight of the treasure nature was entrusting to him was too much for his lonely, still childish spirit, for that richness seemed to infuse him with a responsibility, a duty, and he felt the need to lighten the burden by communicating it to others. But then a strange shyness overcame him, sealing his lips, as if the price of that gift were the melancholy and isolation that came with it, condemning him to enjoy and suffer in silence the bitter and divine drunkenness, incommunicable and ineffable, that flooded his heart and clouded his eyes with tears.

13

First there was the vile and cowardly assassination of Lorca in August of '36. That would be the announcement, the opening salvo signifying everything that was to come: the wake-up call for anyone who had ears and wanted to listen, not the deaf and stubborn ones like him, Cernuda.

He still remembers the pain and anger that he felt when, shortly thereafter, he learned of the despicable manner of his execution, and to this very day, nearly two years later, there were entire nights where he couldn't fall asleep, or if he were to nod off, a recurring dream was there to ensnare him, drowning him, suffocating him: they hounded him, they tortured him, they were always there, on the verge of killing him without ever actually going through with it. He would wake up in the Vullioni's house, shivering, desperate, unable to go back to sleep because the following morning, before dawn, he had to be at the boarding house attending to the Basque children, working with the nurses and assistants, inhaling the smells of death and borax lotions.

Rafael and María Teresa León, Altolaguirre and Aleixandre, Emilio, Pedro, Guillén and Gerardo Diego, José Bergamín and Ramón Gaya, Neruda and Dámaso Alonso, their beloved Concha and Rosa Chacel ... everyone had been horribly afflicted by Lorca's death. Friends and strangers. Fans and critics alike. And so suddenly, too, for it had just been in April, four months before his assassination, that they had all gathered for that memorable meeting which none of them would ever forget: celebrating the first edition of *Reality and Desire* at a restaurant on Calle Botoneras in Madrid. Who would have thought? Who could have imagined at the time that Federico wouldn't with them much longer, at the center of the group, drawing them together like only he (with that delightful, joyful smile of his) could do during difficult times and with such sensitive, thin-skinned people? God, how I loved him!

The second wake-up call came quite suddenly: the court ruling by the Minister of Culture, Wenceslao Roces, censoring *Elegy*, which Cernuda wrote one night in August at an open air café in Cercedilla, not far from Madrid. What right did they have? How dare those fucking politicians and their brown-nosing advisors remove or replace something which, according to their sanctimonious views, chafes with humble, respectable, moral decency, when everyone knew as well as he did that Federico liked men, and from time to time they'd compete for the affection of some young fellow, or even swap them back and forth at Aleixandre's house? What right did those hypocrites have to dictate the customs and manners of an allegedly democratic and falsely Communist Spain? If they'd known in time—if Gil-Albert had at least warned them—they never would have allowed his *Elegy* to García Lorca be published in a ridiculous little volume of *Poets in a Loyal Spain*, no, not at all. But they were late … it was too late by the time news of the suppression had spread. There was nothing to be done about it. Still, though, it should have been an eye-opener, it could have been prevented, and yet I did nothing, Rafa, I decided to continue on blindly, believing in the cause, in the goodness and justice of the cause. Can you believe it? Not content with having just enlisted in the Alpine Batallion and fighting in the Sierra de Guadarrama, I clung to my naïve faith as if it were a secular religion. And I did it because it was the other ones who were the sons of bitches, it *had* to be them, Franco's supporters, the Catholic Fascists. How could it not be them? How the hell could it have been any other way? *Ergo*, Rafa, the Communists *should*, consequently, have been the good and decent men in that story, the heroes and victims of all that horror. And they were, of course … do you know why? Because I was one of them. Do you see now my stupidity, my blindness? It's a simple equation: if I'm good (at least, if I'm not a son of a bitch) and I declare myself a Communist, *ergo* the Communists *are* or *must* be just as decent, principled, and educated. Unable to assassinate anyone. What a joke! Such a fuck up. My God! How did I miss it? Why couldn't I see the diabolic war machine churning on when I was still living in Spain? Just like Alberti and Pablo and Rosa, I thought—we all thought—they were honorable because they were Red, just because of that, you see? Regardless of the gruesome, internal war between the Trotskyites and the Stalinists. I'm so ashamed now to realize how naïve I was back then! I don't know how I'll be able to look you in the face, how I'll be able to talk to you in person, Rafa, or where I found the shame to go on living when there's so much stupidity and horror involved, so much ignorance and shortsightedness. Naïveté is expensive, Rafa. And now I'm paying for it, we're all paying for it, but the one who paid the highest cost of all was of course Federico, and that really isn't fair, it weighs on me, I feel awful every time I think about him, every time I think about his generosity, his complete and utter devotion. Meanwhile, here we are, the survivors, knowing that others died in Spain, betrayed by a lost cause, believing that we mattered to the Russians or that they would be motivated by a sense of altruism or camaraderie. What a worthless word that is, eh? Rafa, this war is fucked because the Soviets, as we now know, will sell cheap weapons for political capital, for our absolute submission to their doctrine, for our devotion to their religion and their party and their universal hatred. That's just another price we pay on top of the thousands upon thousands of deaths. I saw it with my own eyes. I confirmed it back when my gullible young self still believed in the good and selfless intentions of the Party.

"What do you mean, Luis? What did you see?" interrupted Martínez Nadal, reaching for his rapidly cooling cup of tea. As usual, the two of them were seated comfortably in Rafael's flat in Queen's Court. Outside it was cold as hell.

"I'm talking about the Congress of Anti-Fascist Writers in Valencia, remember? Sponsored by our own, overthrown government."

"Of course I remember," Rafael replied. "Even though I wasn't there, it almost feels like I was, Luis. But what did you confirm? I don't understand."

"Despite everything that was going on, Valencia wasn't all bad, since it finally opened my eyes to the truth. I couldn't keep moving forward with the blinders on, with a childlike Manichaean idea of war, distinguishing between the good and the bad, between Catho-

lics and Communists, between Trotskyites and the Stalinists, between Fascists and Reds, when all of them are equally incurable sons
of bitches … with very few exceptions throughout. The problem,
Rafa, lies in the heart of Spain, or perhaps it's in the maggot-ridden
heart of all mankind."

"I don't quite follow …"

"I'm talking about the third motive, the third reason why I broke
with the Reds, with Neruda and Alberti, as much as I liked and
admired them, you know?"

"You'll have to do better than that, Luis."

"When I first learned that the Party had banned Gide from attending the Congress for shouting out the truth, for having the
balls to publish it, I was confused. Banning the bravest among us?
Incredible. And of course, that little book of his which I read time
and again … well, they didn't like it in the least. If it were intended for them, the damn Torquemadas would have burned him at
the stake. Hearing about the atrocities attributed to Stalin couldn't
have pleased the goons within the Party, of course; Gide ruined and
continues to ruin the profitable business of war, the criminal game
wherein one group is supported by many, you see, out for their own
personal gain."

Cernuda paused here to catch his breath, sucking in what seemed
like tons and tons of air. Every time he remembered Federico's vile
assassination, and the subsequent, despotic censorship of the homosexual verse in his *Elegy*, which he'd written in April of the previous
year, was shortly followed by Gide being banned from attending
the Congress in Valencia (also the previous year), and, finally, the
arrest of his friend, the painter Víctor María, he felt sick to his stomach and livid with anger which—much to his embarrassment—he
could scarcely hide. Finally, he took a deep lungful of air, and continued on with Rafael:

"As I said, the thing with Víctor was the straw that broke the
camel's back. For me, that was the fourth and final reason for my
detachment, or should I say my complete separation. That was the
beginning of my complete and total skepticism, which is not to be

confused with cynicism."

"I don't know what happened with Víctor."

"The people from the Ministry of Culture asked Altolaguirre to take charge of La Barraca after Lorca was murdered, remember?"

"Yes, that much I know. Manolo told me about it."

"You know him well: he was delighted with the new task, he would have done it just for the love of it, just as Federico would have. In any case, they decided to put on a production of *Mariana Pineda*. They subsidized us so lavishly that we could, during those few months of previews, throw money around recklessly, go drinking at the Volga night after night ... but then, that's a different story."

"Of course," Martínez Nadal interrupted. "What could be better than exploiting Federico's death for your own benefit?" he mused.

"Exactly, Rafa, you know what I mean. The Ministry of Culture doesn't give a damn about Lorca, his plays, or culture or La Barraca. All they wanted to do was lavish attention on the Congress of Anti-Fascist Writers, as you know. When Manolo asked me if I wanted to play the part of Don Pedro Sotomayor, I said I'd be delighted, and I have no regrets. Those were unforgettable times, and quite entertaining as well, because after the previews we'd go out on the town, drinking and dancing and talking all sorts of rubbish. In any case, Manolo asked Víctor to take charge of the scenery and costumes, and you have no idea how good he is at that sort of thing. The fact is that we opened the play in August, I believe, to welcome the delegation. Orwell, Ehrenburg, Spender, Vallejo, Neruda, Hemingway, Pellicer, Huidobro, Malraux, and many others were in attendance. The cream of the crop, shall we say. Of course, to these cultured politicos, who know nothing of theater, our production was horrific. The sense of surrealism, which is what Cortezo was trying to do with the set design, did not amuse them. In fact (and so this story doesn't go on any longer than need be), I believe that they had developed a bit of a grudge against Víctor María ever since agents from the Military Intelligence Service had found a Bible in his home a few weeks before ..."

"A Bible?"

"That's what I said, Rafa."

"What's wrong with that?"

"Apparently you don't quite realize what sort of people we were dealing with. Those Reds were stark raving mad. Their fanaticism knew no bounds. I don't know which is worse, or who is sicker to the core, I swear ..."

"So what happened, Luis?"

"According to them, that Bible, along with a few chapters of a novel he was writing proved his antirevolutionary tendencies, and that was more than enough to warrant his imprisonment. So, without further ado, they took him away, and there was nothing any of his friends could do about it. And the Ministry washed their hands of it, of course ..."

"They took him away, just like that?"

"Just like the Fascists had done with Federico."

"I can't believe it."

"Fortunately for Víctor, a childhood friend of his, I don't remember the name, was one of the police officers who questioned him. Thanks to that miraculous coincidence, Víctor was acquitted of any wrongdoing and was free to go. But the fear remained. As I said, Rafa, that was the straw that broke the camel's back. At least for me. It was time to take notice and pay attention. After turning a blind eye in the wake of Federico's death, Víctor's interrogation came as a final warning. No Spaniard—however much of a liberal or a leftist you think you are—could tolerate these Communist purges and persecutions, which is how Gide referred to them in his little book. Why stand for this? What purpose does it serve? To earn a spot in the paradise of a Marxist utopia, which is just as false and ideologized as the Christian heaven? Tell me this: what difference is there between the Fascist inquisition and the Red inquisition? Which of the two is more tolerable, the orthodox left or the orthodox right? Neither side inspires me; I fear and despise them both. And to make matters worse, now that I've escaped them, I find myself subjected to the intolerable hospitality of my admirer

and English translator, who saved my life thanks to his insuffer-
able sense of devotion. I don't know what's worse, Rafa, or perhaps
I've just become a crazy old man, irritated by everything." Cernuda
paused here for a few seconds, hesitating because he didn't quite
know how to better express himself, how to define his inextricable
feelings. Then he continued: "Anyway, I told him I'm leaving, and
he started to cry, can you imagine? I had to hug him and beg his
forgiveness, which irritated me even more, and now I find myself in
a completely untenable situation ... untenable because I can't stand
the fact that I come across as a heartless, ungrateful guy."

"Does it matter to you at all that you still love him?"

"No, it's not that. He's important to me, and it bothers me that
I seem like an ingrate," Cernuda clarified. "I can't stand ungratefulness, and truth be told, I don't believe I've behaved that way to such
a degree that he should start crying like a little girl."

"Don't worry about the tears; Stanley is an adult. To me, it
sounds more like blackmail, Luis. A last-minute appeal to keep you
there in his house. But I do also believe that your pressing desire to
leave must have hurt him deeply. I'm not sure whether I'm making
any sense."

"I think I understand."

"Stan believes—as do you and I—in the righteousness of the
Republican cause, no? He even told me once that he wanted to
enlist in the army."

"That's true. He's a believer. But it's more than that: his love for
the country and the Republic is so great that he's started a new book
titled *Poems for Spain*. I suppose it must seem so exotic to be writing
about Spain right now. It's quite the fashion in England. Stan is just
unbearable."

"So? Are they good?" Rafael asked, adjusting his glasses.

"What? The poems?"

"Yes."

"I don't like them at all, quite frankly. What can I say?" confessed
Cernuda, a bit annoyed. "I've read a few, and the poor thing has no
talent for poetry, other than being quite affected and sickly-sweet.

He tries hard, but he writes thinking about other writers—What will they say? How will I be read?—which is exactly the opposite of what an authentic poet should do. What interests me is poetry that says what the poet believes without restrictions, poetry that runs the risk of casting doubt on the importance of a clear conscience. Everything else is tasteless and crude. Stan's new poems about Spain are—if you can believe it, and don't tell him—even worse than the ones in *Dark Blue Sunlight*, which was just published. Have you read them yet?"

"No."

"Don't waste your time, then."

"Madariaga told me they were quite good."

"Forgive me, but what does Don Salvador know about poetry?" Luis blurted out dismissively, knowing full well that Rafael deeply admired the diplomat who, at the time, was working on a draft of his famous novel *The Heart of Jade*.

The two of them fell silent for a few moments. Lola had passed through the room where they were having their discussion. She disappeared.

Finally, steering the conversation in a new direction, Martínez Nadal asked his dear friend, "So yours is now finished, Luis?"

"Fortunately, yes. It has nothing to do with causes, Rafa. Despite the fact that we both share and believe in the same causes of truth and justice, the fact is that I simply and truly cannot bear it. I can't bear it as a man, as a human being. It has to do with love. Or enmity. It deals with another sort of war, a much more complicated one."

14

Luis Salerno picked up the phone and dialed. He listened to it ring once, twice, three times before someone finally answered. It was a woman's voice, a young woman. Was it her? Probably, yes.

He hung up. Scared off the line.

Shit. He was acting like a spineless teenager. Behave yourself. Don't be so nervous. Not now. Jacinto had gotten Amparo's number from her mother (an exceedingly simple task) and now Luis was on the verge of speaking, for the first time in his life, with the woman who might well be his half sister.

He was feeling fainthearted; his hands and knees were trembling. He became aware of his nervousness, of the irregular rhythm of the air in his lungs. He hung up the phone and laid his hands on his thighs to stop that stupid tick of tapping his feet, sitting there in front of the phone as if he were watching some horror film or suspense thriller.

He dialed again. His palms were sweating.

He waited for it to ring, once, twice ... he should hang up, yes, he should hang up right now, but he stopped himself from doing so. He had to stop acting like a wishy-washy teenager. He had to ante up and find the courage to face the voice of the woman on the other end of the line.

Then he heard it again: *her* voice.

"Hello?" she said.

Luis was left silent. He thought he'd said something, but not a word escaped his mouth. Nothing but air, a breath. And the female voice again:

"Yes?"

"Hello," Luis finally said.

"Who's speaking?"

"I'd like to speak with Amparo Salerno, please."

"Speaking. Who is this?"

"I'm Luis."

"Luis who?" But as she was asking the question, Amparo's voice changed, turning just a fraction of a note more acute, more sharp. It was a premonition, and Luis had scarcely an instant in which to vaguely gather that she, this unknown woman, knew exactly who he was: her half brother, her younger half brother. Should Luis say something along the lines of, I'm Luis, your brother? Or better yet, I'm Luis, your half brother? Or should he just offer his last name? He hesitated.

"I know who you are," Amparo said, saving Luis from the complicated task of introducing himself.

"You do?" Luis asked awkwardly, not knowing what else to say.

"Of course. I'm so glad you called ..."

"Are you sure?"

"More than you could imagine."

Luis fell silent for a moment. Should he ask that other question that was begging to explode from his lips, the question he'd been wanting to ask ever since he first learned of her existence? He did it: "Then why haven't you ever called me?"

Amparo paused. Luis knew this could take a few seconds; perhaps he'd gone a bit too far. But finally, he heard the answer:

"It's a long story. But that doesn't matter anymore now, does it?"

"No, it doesn't," Luis lied. Of course it mattered. It would have been fantastic to accept and believe that it didn't (in fact, it was, perhaps, the sanest thing in the world to do), but the reality was that it did matter to Luis, it mattered a lot, although now he couldn't (nor should he) contradict this new sister of his, whom he hadn't ever even seen before. He must consent, he must agree with her in all things. At least for now.

"You're just agreeing with me for my sake," Amparo said suddenly, as if reading his thoughts. "I know."

Luis was petrified. He didn't say a thing.

"Diana and I have been good friends for some time now. Well, we were good friends until she decided just to end it ... like I said, it's a long story."

Luis was still stuck in his stupor. Good friends? How ... they were half sisters? And if they were or are such good friends, why didn't he know anything about this? What happened? This was all exceedingly strange.

"Does Marcela know?"

"No, no she doesn't."

Luis was about to ask if her dad (their father) knew, but it would be pretty ridiculous to pose such a convoluted (if pertinent) question. He preferred to remain silent.

"I know you, Luis. I've seen you several times, but you never knew who I was. I was at Cirilo and Diana's wedding, and before that I saw you at Cirilo's graduation party. You were there with a friend of yours. That's where we spoke for the first time in our lives, just a few words, but even before that, I'd already gone to see you ... I mean, I wanted to get to know you, so I went to your college and watched you from a distance."

"Good lord!" Luis could not contain his astonishment.

"Yes, good lord indeed!" Amparo laughed. "That's why I said I'm really glad that you called. You just can't imagine. It's like a dream come true."

"But if you're so glad, as am I, why didn't you just reach out to me? That's what I don't understand, Amparo. I'm sorry to be so insistent, but I just don't get it."

"I did reach out to you. We even spoke on a couple of occasions. For years now, I've known almost everything about you. I know you're fascinated by movies, photography, art films, that you don't have many friends ..."

Stunned, Luis replied: "But I had no idea ... I didn't even know who you were. How could I, since you never said anything to me?"

"You couldn't."

"So why, then?"

"It's a long story."

Once again, Luis had received that enigmatic and intolerable answer: *it's a long story.* Life itself is a long story.

"I'd like to see you, so we could talk," Luis said, scared to death.

"Sure. I'd like that," she replied.

"Are you married?"

"Yes, I have two daughters. One is thirteen and the other is eleven."

"You must have been young?"

"More or less."

Luis didn't know what else to say, what he could add to all this. All of a sudden, he'd run out of words, but his unanswered questions remained. He was empty, he was filled. He was motionless: his feet, finally, had stopped tapping. Only his hands were sweating.

"Diana asked me to go with her to sell her car in McAllen," Luis finally said. "We're leaving tomorrow. Could I see you on the way back? Let's say Tuesday or Wednesday?"

"Of course. Whenever you like." Then, almost immediately, she asked, "Will you talk with her? Will you tell her that you called me?"

"Good question. I think so. Sooner or later she should know that I know, don't you think?"

"I suppose so," Amparo said, before she once again added a bit of uncertainty: "She might be better at answering the questions you've asked. Yes, I think it would be better if Diana tells you everything."

"But either way, we'll see each other ..."

"Yes, Tuesday or Wednesday. You call me. Promise?"

"I swear."

"Hey ... wait, don't hang up," Amparo said. "How did you get my phone number? How did you find me?"

"It's a long story," Luis joked. "I'll call you on Tuesday, okay? Adiós."

"Adiós."

15

"Do you know what Christ, Saint Francis of Assisi, Nietzsche, and Al Gore have in common?" Jacinto had asked on that occasion. Luis remembered it well; it was just before he left for New York, at a café in La Condesa.

"I have no idea."

"Each of them, in his own way, felt like the savior of humanity: messiahs, gods, redeemers of men. They were obsessed with saving the world, setting it right, despite the fact that there was nothing wrong with it. In fact, it was perfectly fine. However, out of all of them, I think the only one who actually knew why he did what he did was Nietzsche."

"What are you talking about?"

"All the others believed they were motivated by pure altruism, that sense of love or compassion for all."

"And if that wasn't it, what was the motivation?"

"Like I said, only Nietzsche knew that the true motive was egoism . . . a sort of redemptive egoism, sure, but egoism nonetheless. In all other things, the four were identical. They considered themselves the saviors of all mankind. Conscious of his egoism, Nietzsche attacks compassion. He considers it an appalling sentiment, and relies on Spinoza and others to justify his argument. However, and despite all that, Nietzsche still wants to set the world straight. Ultimately, he's an altruistic prophet like Zarathustra."

Luis Salerno Insausti was lost in thought. He didn't know how to respond. Now he remembered. But before he could think it through and develop his reply, Jacinto adjusted his glasses and came to his aid:

"But you know, just yesterday, something derailed my theory. Well, I don't know if it was completely derailed, but it was pretty shaken. It's the first time that's happened since I first accepted it around three years ago. Ever since then, I've been a firm believer in the fact that the world is moved by egoism, despite the fact that of course the world doesn't realize it and instead refers to it as philanthropy, Christian charity, mercy, love, compassion, benevolence, altruism, agape, empathy, or whatever term you prefer."

"So what was it that dealt a blow to your theory, may I ask?" Luis wondered, just to humor him.

"Yesterday I watched a show on TV called *When Weather Changed History*. I was confused by what I saw, Luis."

"And what did you see?"

"In January of 1982, a commercial airliner takes off from Washington Dulles International, and twenty seconds later it crashes into the Potomac River, right near a bridge. Of course, the river is frozen over, and it's snowing hard. The crash breaks through the thick layer of ice, and you can just make out the tail of the plane suspended there, floating above the water. It's four o'clock in the afternoon and as you know, in the winter, it's completely dark by five. So hundreds of people gather along the riverbank and on the bridge to watch when—much to their surprise—they see five survivors clinging to the tail. You heard me, Luis. Out of the two hundred and something passengers and crew, five were out there, floating in the coldest water you could possibly imagine. One of the bystanders records everything, from beginning to end. One of the survivors, a woman, screams frantically, calling for her baby. But of course there is no baby to be found. She, however, had miraculously been saved. The other survivors included three men and another woman; but one of the men was caught up on a part of the plane's tail and would drown two minutes later. The remaining four just float there, unable to move, such is the concreteness of the cold. Finally, fifteen minutes later, amidst the fog, the snow, and the impending darkness that would shred any hope of rescue, a helicopter arrives. The pilot and another man cast a ring buoy to the remaining survivors still clinging to the tail of the plane. First, they drag one of the women to safety on the shore, where a number of ambulances have joined the crowd. One of the other men is saved in the same manner. But then, as they're towing the second woman—the penultimate survivor, the one with the missing child—she faints halfway to the shore, amidst the ice floes. She's losing consciousness, looking crazy or catatonic, her eyes have gone, her body is literally powerless. They've been in the water over twenty minutes now, and hypothermia is threatening to wipe them out at any moment if drowning doesn't do it first. The helicopter hovers five or ten feet over the woman hanging onto or trapped by a large chunk of ice. She's about to go under, but no matter how hard she tries, she can't hook her arm through the ring buoy. Attempt after attempt fails. The video camera is recording everything. Finally, miraculously, she somehow manages to work her arm through the flotation device; the helicopter turns and begins towing her towards the banks of the river, and just then the camera captures the precise moment when the woman, every last bit of energy gone, slips lifelessly from the ring buoy and inevitably sinks beneath the surface of the river."

"Holy shit! That's awful! So what happened next?" Luis lit a cigarette without batting an eyelash.

"Here's what shook up my entire theory, and I saw it yesterday with my own eyes, Luis. Something incredible."

"What?"

"First, this man, a stranger from the crowd that had gathered on the shore, takes off his shoes, gloves, and coat and dives right in to the river, swimming with astonishing speed, which is barely noticeable or perhaps even an illusion because of the frigid, ice-choked water slowing him down, holding him back. I guess the temperature wouldn't let him swim any faster. He knows this, and therefore he can't slacken, he can't lose so much as a second. He literally knows that there's not a second to lose. The woman is already underwater. She's sinking. In the blink of an eye, the unknown man grabs her, pulls her up, lifts her head above the surface so she can breathe, and begins the enormously daunting task of dragging her to shore. But it quickly becomes clear that he's not going to make it. It's too much. The cold numbs everything. It's getting dark. The helicopter hovers uselessly over the ice and water. The people on the shore watch in bewilderment. The rescuer has fallen victim to the cold himself. So another man on the shoreline takes off his shoes and coat and dives in without a second thought, swimming furiously until he reaches the woman, takes her by the head and drags her the rest of the way to the shore, where others are waiting to help. The helicopter crew throws the ring buoy towards the first stranger; he grabs hold, and they drag and tug him back to the shore safe and sound. Then, the helicopter goes back for the last of the survivors, still clinging to the wreckage of the plane's tail section, which was slowly but surely sinking into the river. In the end, Luis, out of the two hundred and some passengers, only four survived."

"What a story! I'd never heard of it before," Salerno remembers saying that afternoon, riveted in his chair at the little café in La Condesa. "So what is it about all this that challenged your theory, Jacinto?"

"Don't you see? If we're motivated only by our own self-interests, then why did those two men risk almost certain death? And on top of that, to save a complete stranger? That's what I don't understand. Anyone would dive into a river to save their mother, their child, their best friend. But why risk your life to save a stranger without any sort of prompting whatsoever, when not even the guy in the helicopter is willing to do so, and that's supposed to be his job? Understand? I can't stop thinking about it. What moved those two men to go, reflexively, to the rescue of that unknown woman? Is it egoism yet again, a biological survival mechanism or an urge to redeem like Christ or Al Gore? I can't stop mulling it over, Luis."

16

Luis's older sister Diana had asked him (a few days before the revelation Jacinto had brought forth at his apartment) to accompany her to McAllen to sell her old American car for a better price. Every year, Diana and her (former) husband had to cross the border to restart the never-ending formality of legalizing the car's paperwork: a truly annoying and perfectly stupid task. Ultimately it had been Cirilo's idea, for he assumed it would be easy to buy a cheaper car in the United States without (of course) factoring in the future costs of each and every trip across the border to be able to legally drive it in Mexico without having the police pull you over every other day and ask for your registration.

When Luis and Diana finally hit the road, days after that meeting in Jacinto's apartment, his older sister still had no idea that her brother already knew about Amparo. Or to be more precise, she had no idea that Luis knew that Diana already knew all about Amparo, and therefore neither could she sense that Luis was secretly furious at having been deceived; rather, at having been cut off (isolated) from the truth and forced to learn about Amparo's existence from his friend's mouth: the most egregious of all the appalling, despicable ironies in his life. Diana drove and Luis drove and still she had no idea. They spent the night in Monterrey, a couple of hours from the border, at the home of his cousin Adriana, the daughter of his father's sister. It was there, that night, during dinner or perhaps dessert, that the truth jumped to life and shattered the windows of the soul.

"Let me explain exactly how it all happened, Luis," Diana said, quite stunned to learn all of a sudden that Jacinto, that son of a bitch friend of her brother's, had revealed the existence of a half sister to Luis, who had been unjustly deceived his entire life, as had their youngest sibling, Marcela. "I've really been wanting to tell you all along."

"But you didn't!" Luis was nearly shouting while Adriana looked on, stunned, sitting there perfectly silent and motionless on the edge of the precipice that was the conversation between her two cousins there in the cool evening on the balcony of her Monterrey home.

"Only because Dad asked me not to. That's why."

"He asked you not to tell me?"

"Look, it all started the day I put that ad up on campus. It was years ago, remember?"

"What ad?"

"The one about selling my VW Bug so I could afford to go to Europe after finishing high school. Cirilo used to buy them, turn them into taxis, and lease them out."

"I already know all that," Luis growled, anxious to get to the point.

"So Cirilo came over, checked out the Bug, and bought it. Later that night, he told his older sister Lucía that he'd met a girl he liked by the name of Diana Salerno Insausti ... that would be me."

"So that's when you found out."

"No, I still didn't know anything at that point. Just wait ..." Diana replied, trying to calm him. She wanted to go one step at a time, justifying her silence and her decision to cover up for her father, and to do so she had to go all the way back to the beginning, to the start of it all. "Cirilo's sister was and still is Amparo's best friend. Ever since they were kids. So Lucía, my former sister-in-law, spoke with Amparo and told her that Cirilo had met us. I don't know if Amparo already knew that her father was also our father, or if that's when she found out, or maybe that was when her mother finally dared to tell her about it. I think she already knew, but it would have been a pretty recent revelation. From what I understand, for Amparo, this whole thing about having a father was new, since for years — her entire childhood and adolescence — her mother had hidden the truth from her. I think she even said, first, that her father was dead, and then that he lived really far away, in another country, and so, with so much doubt, she just grew up not really caring about it until one day — not long before all this that I'm telling you about — she finally decided to really push her mother so hard that — according to what Amparo told me—she finally decided to tell the truth ... that is, *her part* of the truth."

"Meaning Dad was her biological father."

"Yes. That's what her mother said."

"So what else happened?" Luis demanded, spurring the issue forward. He couldn't help but feel more offended, more excluded, with every passing minute during that night in Monterrey.

"Well, just what you know: Cirilo and I started dating, and Amparo, Cirilo, and his sister Lucía all decided not to tell me for almost a year."

"Why?"

"I have no idea. If I had to guess, I'd say first that Cirilo didn't want it interfering with our relationship ... but of course, eventually, as you'll see, he changed his mind and told me everything. Then again, maybe the real reason was that Amparo was afraid and still not ready to come up to me and say, 'So, Diana, it looks like we're sisters ...'"

"So how the hell did it all happen then? How did you find out?"

"I already told you. A year later, when Cirilo asked me to marry him, he also told me that he couldn't go forward with this secret inside him, and that he had to tell me the truth. And of course, I said, 'What truth? What the hell are you talking about?'"

"So that's when he told you."

"Yes."

"But by that time, you already knew her?"

"Actually, yes. I'd seen her a couple of times, that's all. We'd bumped into each other at Cirilo's house, because like I said, his older sister and Amparo had been good friends since they were little."

"So they are both the same age."

"Yes."

"And older than us."

"A couple of years."

"So our half sister was born before Mom and Dad met, and not *after*?"

"Yes."

"Not that it really matters," Luis muttered to himself in a fit of inopportune justification. "I mean, what matters to me — what I can't even conceive of, nor forgive you for, Diana — is finding out that I have a half sister, and later coming to learn that I could have found out years and years earlier, back when you got married."

"You're absolutely right about that, Luis. I know you're angry . . ."

"Of course I'm right. I'm furious. I'm incensed."

"But what you don't know is why I didn't tell you."

"So tell me then."

Sitting between them at the table on the balcony overlooking her yard on that Monterrey night, Adriana couldn't look away; she didn't so much as touch her cup of decaf, too astonished, perhaps, at being fortunate enough to witness such a significant revelation that involved her own uncle, her mother's brother, no less. Would she have known? Her mother? Adriana suddenly thought to herself. Perhaps she would have, for all those years, while at the same time keeping it from her brother. That, however, was a whole other matter.

"When Cirilo told me, Luis, I almost fainted. The very next day, if I remember correctly, I met with Amparo one on one, and we talked at length. Hours and hours. It wasn't easy, believe me. Even now, I'm still not sure what she knew and when she knew it. I don't even think she knows herself. It's all so convoluted."

"I don't understand, Diana. Explain yourself."

"I'm saying that if she knew everything, then why wait two or three years before approaching us, or approaching me, about it? She had no answer for that, she still hasn't explained that part of it to me, or even to herself. First, Amparo told me that every time she asked about her father, her mother would avoid or avert or postpone her questions. And she didn't insist. Maybe deep down, she didn't really want to know. Who knows. She doesn't, not with certainty, anyway. She was so much younger then. It seems, though, that she got a little more emboldened as the years went by, and eventually decided to clear everything up. So she finally confronted her mother one day when she was seventeen or eighteen, something like that. She said, very determined, that she wasn't going to stop until she got a clear and definitive answer about who her father was, since at the end of the day, she told me, 'Everyone has a father, Diana, and to this day, I've contented myself with listening to empty ambiguities.'" Diana paused here for a moment, perhaps recalling some important detail from the past, before continuing. "Once Amparo learned the truth, she says it took her a long time before she worked up the courage to approach Dad, even though she knew full well how to find him from that point on. And then, it seemed as if life itself offered up the chance, the opportune moment, first when Cirilo and I met, then when we got engaged, and finally on the day of his graduation ... In the end, Amparo told me she confronted her biological father at the party my ex-mother-in-law had thrown for Cirilo ..."

"I think I was there," Luis said. "I'm sure of it."

"I was at that party too, Diana. I remember it well," Adriana said, chiming in for the first time in this unforgettable conversation.

"That night, Amparo sat down next to Mom and Dad for at least a couple of hours. Right there on the same couch. And neither of them had any idea that the young woman sitting next to them was none other than our own father's daughter."

"Now you've lost me again," Luis interrupted. "Did he know or didn't he?"

"He knew that he had another child, or he did, many years before that, when Amparo's mother was pregnant, but he had no idea whatsoever that the girl sitting next to him at my fiancé's graduation party was his own biological daughter. That part, he did not know. To the point that it wasn't until Mom got up for a moment to use the bathroom, that Amparo turned to dad and blurted out the truth, her truth: 'Excuse me, but my mother says that you're my dad.' Imagine the look on Dad's face, Luis. As hard as I might try, I just can't picture it. It must have been a huge shock to him, a real bolt out of the blue. He probably couldn't sleep for days after that."

"A very well-deserved shock, I'd say," Luis replied angrily. "So how did Dad respond?"

"First he asked what was her name, then how was her mom doing, how old was she, and maybe something like 'How long have you known,' or 'Have you told your mother,' I don't know. And then, when he saw Mom coming back from the bathroom, he asked for her phone number and promised to call her so they could get together and talk ..."

"So what happened? Did he call?"

"Never."

"Why not?"

"I don't know, Luis. Later on, I asked him about it, but he didn't answer me. He couldn't."

"That despicable coward!" Luis exploded.

"Don't call him that."

"I'll call him whatever the hell I feel like calling him. You can't tell me how to address that man."

"That man is your father," Diana countered, "and a very good one at that ..."

"He hasn't been a very good one to Amparo ..."

Adriana sensed that now was the time to offer them a couple of glasses of Baileys on the rocks, which she did quickly, without waiting for confirmation from her cousins. Fortunately, the night was cool, and the only audible sound on the balcony overlooking the yard was that of the screeching cicadas. The silhouette of the mountains, not too far off in the distance, was traced in sinuous, violet lines against the darkness.

"So what happened after the party?" Luis asked, taking a sip of Baileys.

"Like I told you, Cirilo felt compelled to tell me the truth. Since Amparo still hadn't found the courage to approach me or any of us about it, Cirilo did it for her."

"Of course she hadn't, especially after that utter disaster, that bucket of ice water her own father threw in her face."

"Maybe that's why. I don't know."

"She would have been hurt," agreed Adriana.

"Just imagine, Adriana," Luis said, addressing his cousin for the first time, "how hard, how difficult it must have been for that young woman to actually speak to her biological father after years and years of lies and setbacks, and then all she gets in terms of a response is the false promise of a phone call. I can't believe it. It's just not fair, damn it! I don't understand Dad, frankly. How hard could it have been to sit down with her and talk, just talk? You said yourself that he never called."

"That's what she told me."

"Something fishy is obviously going on here, Diana, don't you realize it?"

"I don't understand."

"First of all, it's clear that Amparo is our dad's daughter ..."

"Well, it's not clear to me," refuted Diana.

"Because you don't want to see it. That's why. What other way is there to interpret our father's actions, or rather, his inactions? Tell me. If you've got nothing to hide, you've got nothing to fear. And he broke his word when he failed to call. Our dad could easily have sat down and spoken with her, told her that she was wrong, explained himself, his reasons, his part of the story ..."

"But wait, that happened."

"When?"

"A long time later."

"When?"

"When she went looking for him again, about a year later."

"A year, you say?" Luis protested, standing halfway up out of his chair.

"Or more."

"And with all that, you still don't think our father behaved like an asshole?"

"I already told you not to talk about our dad like that."

"In any case, you already knew ..."

"I found out after the fact."

"What do you mean, after the fact?"

"After the graduation party, and before I married Cirilo. Seven or eight months after our father failed to fulfill his promise. After seeing Amparo, his sister Lucía's best friend, so anxious, depressed, barely eating anything, waiting for that call through long, sleepless nights, Cirilo decided he couldn't go through with the wedding if he were hiding the truth from me. So he told me, and—like I told you—I'd seen Amparo on maybe five or six times in my entire life. This time, of course, it was a completely different situation."

"As sisters," Adriana said.

"Well, I don't know about that," Diana replied. "I still don't know whether Amparo is my half sister or not."

"How can you be so completely blind, Diana!" Luis argued angrily.

"But you don't know either. How can you be so sure?"

"I don't need to see her or meet her to know, okay? It's that simple. All I needed was to hear it from Jacinto's mouth, and I knew, at that exact moment, that I'd been living a lie perpetrated by my own father ... and by extension, by you, his disgraceful partner in crime ... I don't need a DNA test, I don't need to see the resemblance, and I don't need to hear it from my own dad. I know it. My intuition plus the facts confirms it for me. I can feel it running through my veins. That's all there is to it. No mother—no matter how crazy she might be—lies to her daughter about the identity of her own father. It just doesn't make any sense. I believe that lady more than I do my own father. Pure and simple. Where there's smoke, there's fire."

"Don't be an idiot."

"You're the idiot, for deceiving Marcela and me for all these years, and for aiding and abetting Dad's lies."

"But you don't know what it was like ... you don't know what happened ..." Diana stammered, breaking into tears.

"Well I'm all ears now! Spit it out!" Luis was almost screaming, paying no mind to his sister's tears. "I'm listening!"

"Dad was on his knees, begging me not to tell anyone, not you, not Marcela, and not Mom."

"What?" Luis demanded, nearing his boiling point.

"You heard me. When I went to talk to Dad, I knew that Cirilo had already gone to see him. He told him he was going to tell me everything, that he couldn't go on lying to me, and—by the way—he couldn't go on watching Amparo suffering the way she was. Cirilo told our dad that it wasn't fair to keep the truth from me, and that he truly loved me. That's what he told me, and after that I spoke with Amparo and then with Dad. It all happened shortly before my wedding."

"So was Amparo at your wedding?" Adriana asked.

"Of course. But by then, I had already started to distance myself from her."

"What for?" Luis asked.

"Because our father had assured me that she wasn't his daughter. He told me that he'd met Amparo's mother two or three years before he met mom, but he wasn't the father of her child. That would be Guillermo, a mutual friend, who later turned out to be bisexual."

"What does that have to do with anything?"

"Nothing. Really, nothing at all. Just that Dad assured me that Amparo's mother had wanted him to be the father of her child even before she was born. In other words, since she wasn't going to marry or even have a future with a guy like Guillermo, she picked the dumbest member of their circle of friends—him, Dad—to act as something of an adoptive parent for her future child."

"I don't believe it," Luis snapped, indignant. "That's nothing but a bunch of low down, deceptive hairsplitting, just an excuse to get you off his back and sidestep his own responsibility."

"Well I happen to believe it," Diana countered, blowing her nose.

They all fell silent for a minute or more. Adriana lit a cigarette, offered one to her two cousins, and took a few puffs before Diana added:

"Apparently, a couple months later, Amparo's grandfather sent for our father, and they met in his office with Guillermo, the one true witness to what had really happened."

"So Dad didn't sleep with Amparo's mother?"

"That's what he said."

"Something still doesn't make sense, Diana. Let me lay it out again. Why would Amparo's mother tell her that our dad is her father? Why lie to her? What's her motive? And most of all, why, after so many years?"

"I don't know."

"Well I do."

"You think you know everything, Luis."

"Not everything, but I do know this: Dad misled you, and you were only too willing to be led down that path. That way you wouldn't have to deal with your new headache, am I right?"

"You always see the worst in people. You've got something against dad. You always have, and it's all because you don't think like he does."

"I don't have anything against him, except for the fact he begged you to keep silent all these years and hide the truth from us. Does that seem like no big deal to you? For your information, it's called 'collusion.' What you did is a despicable act of collusion by holding back information that Marcela, our mother, and I deserved to know as soon as you found out."

"But I told you Dad was on his knees, crying, I'd never seen him like that before. How could I not promise to keep quiet about everything, especially when he swore to me that nothing had ever happened between him and that woman, and that Amparo had been lied to by her own mother? I believed him. I still believe him, and that's why I asked her to never again reach out to the three of us."

Suddenly furious thanks to this new discovery, Luis crushed his cigarette on the floor like a bug and said, "You're so pathetic. Look, I can understand how you fell for his pack of lies, especially if I can picture the whole, humiliating scene: the noble, sacred father on his knees, pleading with you to keep some privileged information quiet. But what I still don't quite get is that now you're saying, in front of Adriana and me, that you still continue to believe this coward. And what's more ..." Here Luis raised his voice to an almost shrieking pitch: "What I won't tolerate is that the cost of this sick conspiracy was keeping our half sister away from us. Who the hell do you think you are? What fucking right do you have to decide what to hide and what to reveal when it comes to Marcela and me, when it's our business, too, when it has to do with my own life, my entire existence? If Dad doesn't want or never knew how to be responsible for his daughter, that's his own damn problem for him and his own worthless conscience to deal with, but that doesn't give him or you the right to withhold information that Marcela, Mom and I deserve to know. Is that clear? Do you understand, or is your brain still shut off? It's up to me and my own preconceived notions, it's up to me to decide whether or not to accept her as a sister. Who the hell are you to decide whether I have a right to know? You're nobody, that's who."

"Luis, calm down, please ..." Adriana said suddenly, taking his arm.

Ignoring his cousin, Luis let out one final thundering retort:

"And what's more, what right do you have to keep Amparo away from her two siblings, Marcela and me? Just who the hell do you think you are?"

"Dad asked me ..."

"Fuck him. I'm talking about you, Diana. Just you. Stop hiding behind him and what he asked you to do or not do. Take some responsibility for your own actions, damn it! Own up to your own decisions."

"You really want to talk about me?" This time it was Diana who was raising her voice, forcing her words through her bawling, blubbering tears. "Okay Luis, let me put it to you like this: I don't have room for another sister in my life. I don't want another one. Regardless of what Dad did or didn't do, what he said or didn't say, it's me—you hear me?—I'm the one who doesn't want to hear about Amparo. I'm the one who doesn't want another sister. I can't take it. It's just too much for me."

After listening to what she had to say, gauging the gravity and weight of her words, Luis replied with the same alarming clarity:

"Well it's not too much for me. On the contrary ... I'm perfectly happy about it. I haven't even met her, and I'm already filled with fucking joy. Just so you know. And I'm sure that Amparo has a bigger heart than you too. Why wouldn't I want to get to know a sister with more feelings and a deeper sense of humanity than you, Diana? Come on, answer me. Let's have it."

And with that, Luis walked out of his cousin's house, exultant or enraged or some combination of the two. He wasn't even sure himself. At least he'd shed the pain that had provoked what he considered a cunning betrayal by his sister. Caught quite unawares, Adriana could do nothing but embrace and comfort Diana, who was sobbing uncontrollably after enduring the barrage of insults from her brother.

After that night in Monterrey, Luis never saw Diana again. He didn't go with her to McAllen to sell her car as promised. Instead, he returned to Mexico City to confront his father once and for all.

17

After sending the email to Marcela, Luis checked his inbox for the sixth time that lonely night: there was a new message from Jacinto. With the sweet taste of Turkish coffee still fresh on his lips, he opened it on the spot:

Hey man,

What's up with you? I emailed you two days ago and you still haven't responded. What's going on? Don't you check your messages? Are you pissed at me, or just at the world in general, like always? Anyway, here's the deal: I got inspired yesterday and magically ended up with this long poem. I'm calling it "Sermon" and you'll see why. As soon as you read it, tell me honestly whether you like it or not. Of course, it's got an epigraph from that philosopher you made me read years ago, remember? Before you got the hell out of Mexico. Yes, it's your beloved Karl Popper. It's an ad hoc quote but I really think it goes well with what I'm saying in this long, versicular sermon of mine, which is the crown jewel of my poetic corpus. See what you think. Hope your eyes don't get tired, and write me back you lazy bastard.

Sending hugs from the City of Palaces, and her thirty million caged beasts,

Zarathustra

His friend hadn't even asked how he was doing, what he'd been up to, or how the short film that he'd been planning on shooting in Central Park for several weeks now was coming along. None of that seemed to matter to Jacinto; only (of course) his poetry, his finances, his amorous affairs. Luis hadn't replied to the previous email, it's true, since his best friend had become a bit tiresome, growing less and less interested in anything other than himself, as if he, Jacinto, were the center of the universe, and nothing around him mattered much at all. Nevertheless, he opened the attachment, lit up a new cigarette and began to read his friend's poem on that nearly crepuscular night:

Sermon of the Children

"Whether we should accept the morality of the future just because it is the morality of the future, this in itself is just a moral problem. The fundamental decision cannot be derived from any knowledge of the future."
— Karl Popper

I

Children of the world, listen:
this is over.

Children of the world, true heroes of the world,
I have come bearing good news:
this is over.

What greater discovery, my children,
than to know
— as I sense here today —
that nothing comes after *this*
and that *this* will inevitably end:
there is no heaven, nor Gehenna, nor nirvana,
no limbo, nor Hades, nor Avernus?

There is nothing.

Such peace, so much infinite peace,
what a delight it is to know this,
such joy to live and believe it!
You'll see.

Children of the world, children with fear, listen;
hungry children,
starving children,
suffering children whose needs I have never known;
orphaned children,
victimized children, raped by your uncles, your fathers,
molested children, abused children, listen near and far;
forlorn children, forsaken children,
woeful children, wounded children,
amputees and children with leukemia,
children in chains, children being suppressed,
child laborers, and children under duress,
from the child soldiers in Uganda,
to the child scavengers in Chiapas,
listen to me,
I have come bearing good news:
this is over, *this* is done, and nothing beside remains.
Do you see? Nothing at all.
What happiness! What greater hope and comfort
    could there be!
Think: what greater joy has the world known?
Tell me, children: why would you want Eternal Life?
Why would anyone want to have Eternal Life?

Perhaps to remember this?

Children of the world, true heroes of the world,
happy children of Mother Earth, beloved,

wanted by their parents, suckled and fed,
children healthy and educated,
children, as you play together, listen;

you children, who study and go to school,
you children, who eat to your heart's content, who have never
    known or even   dreamt of hunger,
you children who ride bicycles down the street and receive gifts,
you children who sleep safe and sound, tucked under
    your sheets,
children with families, children with friends, children
    with no fear, listen:
this is over, *this* is done, and nothing beside remains.
Do you see? Nothing at all.
So enjoy, laugh loudly, and learn all that you can,
for soon, there is nothing, nothing at all.
What happiness! What comfort, what greater hope
    could there be
than to give thanks for your fortunate ways,
knowing everything is at hand, and yet it ceases to be …
and that just *because* it ends and wastes away
you can feel (fully) such intense joy today
and is it not a lovely and wonderful way to be?
Think, for a moment, if not …
Think for a moment: what worldly joy could be true if *this*
    does not decay?
What true enjoyment can there be if nothing ever ends,
if what's yours and mine will never pass away?

Now tell me, my children:
why would you want Eternal Life?
Why would anyone want to have Eternal Life?
Perhaps to long for the goodness in this one?

Children of the world, true heroes of the world,
hear the good news and rejoice:
whatever you fear, whatever the horror, the hunger,
    the solitude or suffering,
whenever your happiness fades, when your innocence,
    your confidence, or sleep   begins to wane,
know that it stems from the wars your fathers fought
    on blind faith,
freedom fighters waging wars of soul salvation,
from a religion (by any other name) which promises us
    a Hereafter,
that imposes or seduces you with a Hereafter.
See it, understand it: it triggers the illusion of Future,
produced by the anguish of a better Tomorrow,
caused by dreaming about Eternal Life and wasting time
    meditating on it ...
when, on the contrary, I say unto you with joy:
hurrah ...
this is over, *this* is done,
and nothing beside remains.

II

Children, listen to me well:
you must not waste one second on living for tomorrow,
you must not waste one moment of life on occupying heaven
    or avoiding the inferno ...
which, let it be known, do not exist, despite it all.
O children, my children, they are not even worth the thought.

Children of the world, true heroes of the world,
listen to the poor mystic of today, and not the mystic
    of tomorrow:
I was a Christian until I discovered the Church and Saint Paul.
Yes, through a tiny crack, I stealthily made my way:
I caught a glimpse of his tattered rags, I understood instantly,

and there is nothing more to say.
Children, I swear to you, it was not through force of habit,
but rather the burning desire to reconcile reason with faith,
that I continued to believe in God for awhile,
but one afternoon, I ceased to believe anymore,
something like scales fell from my eyes ...
and this, my children, in and of itself, is neither bad nor good.

Listen well: I will not say to you that God is dead
    or does not exist,
I know nothing of this, which is as much as anyone knows to
    the contrary;
I will simply say, I believe no more, and the profundity of that,
let it be known,
has granted me ineffable relief and an immense gift,
as well as a bit of solace: call it calmness, peaceful acceptance ...
and it is the fine pleasure of discerning, just as I suspected,
that there is nothing, and that *this* is simply over.

Children of the world, true heroes of the world,
know also that, a few years after what I've said here,
I stopped loving Jesus of Galilee.
Do you know why I ceased to love the beloved one?
Because, despite his benevolence and grandeur,
he dared to say we would be blessed if we learned to live today
    as if for tomorrow,
if we exist today as if for the Future,
a Future that is not, was not, nor will be;
the good Jesus insisted on denying you this world ...
however, what I say to you now,
is that you mustn't waste one second living for tomorrow
because joy and misery,
the horror and serenity of the Earth,
the love or the fury,
the wealth or the poverty in this world,

the injustice or the equality in this world,
the days of hunger and the days of plenty,
are only for now, and with this world, will end.

18

1616. Cervantes dies, Shakespeare dies.

1616. That was the name that ended up winning out over the other suggestions offered by Manolo and Concha Altolaguirre for their bilingual poetry journal, a true paragon of virtue, a truly wonderful gem. He had to admit, it was also a quite fortuitous coincidence, a simple and eloquent title, especially for a bilingual poetry journal. And that was or would have been its title during its short life between 1934 and 1935.

As always, spurred by Manolo's daring kindness (along with that of his wife, who supported him in everything) he ventured into this brave undertaking, and as soon as he did so, he reached the same lofty levels of poetic production as his fellow travelers: some of them were friends (like Lorca, Aleixandre, and Altolaguirre himself), some were old friends (like Salinas or Prados), some weren't so friendly (like Diego and Guillén), and others (like Dámaso) who were outright enemies, or at least people whom he despised with all his heart. But the fact was, once again, Luis said to himself, thanks to poetry or to friendship (or thanks to the deceptiveness of fate) he had not died in Spain but lived on in England, reluctantly and against his will. And for what? How and why? He chuckled to himself as he began to connect the dots, to link the coincidences (or should we call them causalities?) together, to complete the puzzle that had brought him into this damn guest room off in the English countryside surrounded by those abandoned children that broke his heart each and every day he visited them and whom he tried — stubbornly, diligently — to help. The truth was that if Manolo and Concha hadn't asked him to look after their flat on Calle Viriato in Madrid (or was it he who offered to stay there under the guise of taking care of it?) the couple would never have gone to London. And without having set foot in that city, it is much less likely (according to Concha) that they would have had the opportunity to publish that lovely bilingual poetry review with Spanish and English variations of all the poems, and—consequently—they wouldn't have needed contributors, and thus wouldn't have met Stanley. It is also thanks to Manolo that Stan arrived in Madrid in March of '34 with the collection of letters of introduction that he always kept with him and which were often presented by several other members of his generation. And out of all of them, it was he and Lorca who welcomed him and showed him all around Madrid, they lavished him with attention in Chueca and several times they took him to dinner at Recoletos or Sol, and eventually it was he who ended up falling in love with Stanley Richardson and not Federico, just as had happened two years prior with Serafín, Manolo's young linotype operator from Galicia. In that sense there was no denying the fact that the two of them, Federico and he, were lucky: they never competed over the same man. Perhaps that was why their friendship was so durable and their affection so deep, yes, it was a perfect camaraderie up until the damn day when the flaming Fascists cut short his life.

Now, he remembers the specific night on which he, along with Federico and Vicente, arrived at the meeting in question with Carlos Morla Lynch, the brilliant new Chilean diplomat who admired him so much and yet understood so little of his poetry. He remembers the exact moment he'd introduced them, and even the precise second when he'd shook hands with Stanley and knew (in a powerful flash of intuition) that soon enough he would want him. And now he also recalls how he realized, almost immediately, that Stan had been sent directly to him. He didn't know whether Manolo had sent him *ex professo* or by divine grace, but he was definitely meant for him, for his pleasure, for his love. He could never have imagined at the time that this messenger with the golden wings was to convert him, much to his ill fortune, into a real angel of providence barely four years later, when he snatched him from the jaws of war.

In any case, a short while after, once the group of friends had dispersed throughout Morla Lynch's flat, Federico discreetly snuck into the corner where Luis was waiting for Stan to return with a couple glasses of wine, and whispered in his ear:

"I think he likes you."

Luis, of course, knew better than to hide things (especially from Federico), and so he simply replied,

"You think?"

"I think so, and don't worry about me, Luis. He's not my type."

"Not mine either." And that much was true: he liked them younger, much younger, with bronzed skin, toasted by the sun, dark and lean, like they are in Málaga, Almería, Cádiz, in short: Andalusian, like him, with less robust bodies and smooth, slender arms, boys with a feminine torso and strong legs though not as muscular as Stanley's legs evidently were, along with his sturdy, athletic arms and shoulders. Nor was he attracted to the nearly albino skin, since the fact was that up to that point he had only known (and kissed) the darker, sloe-colored skin of his own people: the lovely skin of the boys from the south, occasionally a bit flaxen, as it they be in Toledo or the Basque region, but certainly nothing lighter than that. Richardson, however, was blonde, very blonde, with limpid, bright blue eyes: a true denizen of Albion, for sure. How could he sleep with him, to kiss those thin, distinct lips, that pale strongly built body, to hold his member in his hands, his mouth, sucking and loving it? Would it be enjoyable? What would it be like? As pleasing, perhaps, as it was with Serafín? But soon enough—just a few days later, in fact—he would find out.

In the end, it lasted a matter of months, just a few months of unbound lust the likes of which he hadn't felt in a long time, at least since things had ended (amidst jealousy and angst) with Serafín, who was more of a trophy than a true lover. He would caress Stan and let Stan caress him every night after vehemently making love; later they would kiss and cuddle again after having been rendered defenseless there between the sheets of Manolo and Concha's bed on Calle Viriato. Then, in the mornings, it was more of the same, unflagging and relentless: fondling and licking during the lovemaking, as well as before and after. So when would they rest? When would their tongues and taste buds stop enjoying each other, stop producing saliva? When would their mouths dry up?

Soon. Too soon. At least for him. His Andalusian mouth ran

ELOY URROZ

dry as the summer passed, and the passion and desire faded for him
long before it did for Stanley (for it was now clear that Stan's longing and love had not waned even in the slightest during the four
intervening years). Cernuda did not know what, exactly, had happened, why this sudden sense of indifference had occurred, or—if
he did know—he lacked the precise words with which to explain it
to himself, let alone to Stan. It wasn't a linguistic problem. It was a
problem, pure and simple. That's how it was. Passion has no name,
and neither does the death of that passion. Period. And while he
didn't want to hurt him, he didn't want to spend even one more day
with him. He no longer wanted to bring him back to his borrowed
flat on Viriato, to join him for dinner at Recoletos, or even go to
Morla Lynch's house together. The romance, all told, only lasted for
a couple of months, a lapse of time and judgment he could tolerate
no more, and which was quite short when compared with the dura-
tion of his relationship with Serafín, or with the swath the young
Galician man had cut through his life. Did the relationship last until Richardson returned to England, or did it end before that? He
couldn't even remember with certainty. All he knew was that there
was something about Stan that didn't complete him, that wasn't as
fulfilling as it had been in the beginning, when they'd first met.
Something about him didn't click with his sense of self, with his
own, complicated, Sevillian Spanish self, despite poor Richardson's
efforts to please and entertain, to surrender himself completely to
him. And it was this lack of grace (or the grace of a supposed dandy)
that ultimately caused his love to crumble. However, all of that was
still a few months away. That particular night, at the home of the
Chilean Morla, as he took Federico by the shoulder, he couldn't
possibly have imagined that three days later he would be writing
that young Englishman a secret poem which Federico and Vicente
Aleixandre would praise enthusiastically, and which the latter would
later ask him to read aloud at his house on Calle Velintonia for a
select group of people.

The poem was titled *All For Some Yellow Tulips*, and it began as
such:

Swallowing sleep behind a pane of impalpable glass,
Between the twin throats
Of laziness and custom,
I was living in a country in the bright south
When some god's happy message struck me,
Some young scent,
A brimming breath of unexpected warmth.

19

"But how much do you really love the world, Jacinto? How much do you truly love mankind?"

Those were, perhaps, the good times, when he, Salerno Insausti, and his best friend would while away the hours, days, and weeks discussing and lambasting one another regarding their respective philosophical theories and ideas, like the unwonted egoism of Al Gore, Christ, Saint Francis of Assisi, and Nietzsche. What moved them both to such obstinate argumentativeness? Convincing the other? Of course not. Influencing the other? Even less so. Regardless, influence was happening and—in spite of themselves—there was no need for heated exchanges. It was enough, for example, to go to the movies together, to go to a party, or read the same author, and the reciprocal influence would unfailingly arise. They each knew full well what Dawkins's memes signified, and they understood the replication of whatever theory (or idiocy) that one might repeat to the other. Daniel Gilbert, a psychologist whom Salerno admired, used Dawkins's theory to discuss true or false beliefs and how these beliefs are later able to self-replicate as part of man's ability to communicate. So, was it about displaying one's argumentative talents to the other, or just for the pure amusement of it all? Neither. Each of them believed himself to be slightly superior to the other, despite each recognizing much talent and a touch of genius in his friend. Most likely, and without even realizing it, each was basically doing nothing but talking to himself. The other one, being more than just a participant, served as a screen or a mirror, a true extension of ideas and life: that is, an analyst. At least, that's what Luis thinks now, many years later, sitting in his cramped Manhattan apartment, after having read Jacinto's long poem-sermon.

"Loving humanity? What the fuck are you talking about? You come up with the craziest stuff, Luis ..."

"That you're willing to sacrifice your secret paternal desires for the sake of the world. That's what I'm talking about."

"And where did you get that stupid conclusion?" Jacinto said, bewildered, on that distant afternoon in his Mexico City apartment. "I've told you a thousand times what I think about the world; or rather, about the people who populate this world ... the worst. My contempt couldn't run any higher. That's what I think."

"I'm of the same opinion, as you know: the human species is the son of an inveterate bitch. Plain and simple. Man is a wolf to his fellow man." Luis chuckled at his own trite cliché.

"Human beings have to tame themselves. We are bloodthirsty, we're cruel and bloodthirsty, and we have to be vigilant about one another, as your beloved Popper called for ... yes, it's our responsibility as citizens of the world to be ever alert because, at any moment, we are capable of harassing and even destroying one another simply on a whim. Remember those three Spanish teenagers, thirteen, fifteen, and sixteen years old, barely old enough to shave? They first set themselves about the task of kidnapping that young mentally retarded kid, then the three of them raped her before running her over with a car and finally burning her alive. And for what? Because we're just a bunch of sons of bitches if we're not domesticated from a very young age. Right there, in post-Franco, democratic Spain, three kids, three monsters: Mengele, Barbie, and Eichmann. And what distinguishes them from the others? Only the fact that, if they could, they would have gutted and raped an entire school of mentally retarded students. It's just that simple, Luis. It has been proven, observed, and scientifically confirmed ever since we ceased to be higher primates. At that exact moment, millions of years ago, we became monsters. I don't know how it happened, but it did. I suppose that, ultimately, it's an evolutionary question, one that hasn't been studied in depth. We are something much worse than the malevolent wolves you mentioned."

"And that is precisely why I don't understand you. It would seem that deep down you actually love this abominable world with all your heart, despite its wickedness, despite the fact you recognize its intrinsic vileness. It's not just wishful thinking on your part. It's as if you'd like to sacrifice yourself—or sacrifice your biological impetus—

at the altar of evil plaguing mankind."

"That's precisely why I don't have any children, Luis. But in no way does that imply a sacrifice of any kind ..."

"For someone who's as anti-Christian as you say you are, you have a rather backhanded way of being Christian, you know, Jacinto? Actually, you're a lot like Tikhon, that bishop in *The Demons*, who says to the troubled Stavrogin in his monastic cell, 'By sinning, every man has also sinned against all other men, and everyone is at least in part to blame for the sin of others.' Deep down, you feel responsible for the sins of all men, and you also feel responsible for all the children who are born and become evil as all hell, and you don't want to contribute even a whit to that universal, congenital iniquity. That's it."

Jacinto couldn't help a sarcastic chuckle, and then replied while nervously adjusting his glasses, which were constantly sliding down his nose:

"So now I'm some sort of Dostoyevskian monk because I don't want to have kids?"

"More or less," Luis laughed derisively, before adding almost immediately: "No, you're not exactly a Russian monk. However, one thing is true: if you don't truly love this world which, 'in theory,' you say you abhor, you're not really sacrificing all that much. Do you understand the paradox of your entire secular existence?"

"But I don't want to be a parent. I don't want to be anyone's father. It's really quite simple. Are you just not getting it, Luis? It doesn't interest me. I never had that desire that you have, that tickling or itching noogenic or biologic need, whatever you want to call it. I just don't want to bring children into this world ... because, among other things, it's true, this world is a serious piece of shit and it's not worth the pain to bring them here to suffer for no reason, or worse, because nobody deserves to have me unleash a couple of tiny little monsters to inflict gratuitous suffering on the weak simply because they can't find the way to love and be loved."

"Don't you see that I'm right?"

"You're using deceptive words. Or rather, it's how you're using them."

"No," Luis refuted. "You have said yourself, on a number of occasions, that—if the situation arose, and if your wife called for it—you would be willing to adopt. Isn't that true? And haven't you also said that there is no need to bring more little ones into the world, that you shouldn't engender any more when there are already so many abused and orphaned children? Well then, let me say this: if that's not a sacrifice—if that isn't beating back your biological paternal instincts and replacing them with adoption, and if everything I'm describing isn't, ultimately, a way of offering up your own genetic impulse for the sake of this world that you love so much, however 'abominable' you may find it—then what the hell is it?"

"There's just no way to talk to you. You're ideological to the core, except for the fact that whenever you can, you arm yourself with a ridiculous amount of gibberish."

"That's what you always say whenever you run out of new ideas to wield," Luis laughed on that typical afternoon. "The problem, or lack of a problem, is that you love this world too much because you're doing so well in it, because it's been pretty good to you, and because you've known how to make it suit your needs, or rather, because you've made the world suit you, which in this case is the same thing."

"No it isn't."

"Fine, fine ... it's not the same, but let's not get off topic, Jacinto. What I'm trying to say is that achieving what you've achieved is no small feat. On the contrary, your work or self-analysis has cost you. What happens, though, is that you're terrified of taking responsibility for a life that might not turn out as well as yours did in a world where the vast majority of lives don't experience anything good at all. You're the standard, the measure for happiness, and you're imposing that on all the future adults in the world. Everyone else is pretty much fucked, from your perspective, of course. You can't even begin to imagine how someone else might be happy in his own particular way. Finding out, for example, that this hypothetical kid you've brought into the world is struggling financially, suffering from depression, or is a complete failure, unemployed with no friends and no partner … that teenager, I repeat, would come to ruin your cozy sense of happiness, no matter how hard you try to deny his entire existence, which, of course, you would never be able to do, owing, I suppose, to your tortuous, ultra-compassionate, Christian ethics. You couldn't do it, Jacinto, you're just too guilty and too responsible to all the others out there to be able to do it. That's why I say you're a monk, if not exactly an orthodox one. You've become something of an egoistic, atheistic monk who's always in a bitchy mood, but an overly sensitive monk as well, because of your high degree of gratuitous responsibility, a Kantian monk who rants against humanity while at the same time doing an extraordinary job of brainwashing that consists of demonstrating to himself that bringing a child into this world would, once and for all, have a devastating double effect: first, for the world (which has no need for yet another child), and second, for the child itself, who never asked to be a part of this abominable place called Earth. Damn it, what greater ploy, what greater reason, I say, for anesthetizing any inklings of parental desire that might creep up and startle you on melancholy nights of solitude, Jacinto? You're a genius when it comes to fooling yourself with reason."

20

Not having fully digested Jacinto's long poem-sermon, overwhelmed after having read it and not knowing quite how to respond to his friend, Luis got up from his chair, threw on a coat, and got himself ready to wander the streets, for no reason, and—what was even worse—without hunger or thirst. He walked down the five floors of the building without noticing anything, absorbed, like a sleepwalker; however, as soon as he opened the door and a gust of freezing wind slapped him in the face, Salerno came to his senses and decided against walking aimlessly around Manhattan. Better just to stay at home. He had no reason to be out that night, and on the other hand, the next day he would be meeting with the two young actresses who had agreed to participate in his short film just for the love of the art, and in the hopes that one day this young Mexican director would become the next González Iñárritu and remember them for future casting calls (in other words, in the hopes of a cinematic miracle).

Once he was back in his apartment, and after pondering things a bit longer, Salerno decided to fire up his computer and check his inbox; next he searched for the email from the unknown woman (or man), and finally drew the cursor over the "Reply" button. Then he began to write back to the alleged Rosa or whomever that cyber joker really was:

"Excuse me, but who are you?"

A few seconds later, he edited and corrected his message, leaving only the concise question on the screen:

"Who are you?"

Yes, that was more than sufficient. If she (or he) wanted to be laconic in her (or his) emails, then he would be as well.

He clicked the mouse and sent it.

Immediately he felt a great and strange sense of relief: it was as if he had been carrying a huge weight around on his shoulders, and he hadn't even been aware of it until that very moment.

21

Finally, on the ides of March of 1938, Cernuda managed to end things with Stan, who—in return, and to make matters and ironies worse—remained true to his word and set him up with a job working with the homeless, displaced Basque children through the Arden Society for Artists and Writers Exiled in England, an irritating job that Luis did not want but nevertheless needed after his failed attempts at becoming a lecturer at Oxford and Cambridge. His limited English and the poor Spanish spoken by the British graduate students had made communication impossible, save for the purely symbolic paychecks he received: a pittance that wasn't even enough to buy a loaf of bread and a decent bottle of wine, let alone pay rent, however modest it may have been. London, he now knew, was outrageously expensive. The supposed lecture circuit around England that Richardson had organized never materialized; in the end, it turned out to be pure pretense: an unpaid tour with the ulterior objective of getting closer to him (trapping him) while at the same time getting him further away from the war (and death).

Still in Richardson's home, during those final few days under house arrest with his blonde-haired lover, he put all of his effort into translating to English those poems that they both had been working on for the anthology of new Spanish poetry, another project that would ultimately never come to fruition. Maybe it was the marked differences in tone, in timbre, or in pitch that cropped up time and again between one verse and the next, between adjectives and their lexical equivalents, even the syllabic accentuations on which they could never agree, gradually undermining their relationship, which had already been rather unsatisfactory ever since Luis had arrived in England in late February. Despite all that, two of Wordsworth's sonnets had been translated and published in *Hora de España* thanks to that intense collaboration. But now, though, truth be told, none of that mattered much: Cernuda had fled from London (read: Stan) which incidentally put an end to the anthology which the generous

Catalan editor Juan Gili was excitedly awaiting.

However, and despite having achieved what he most wanted, Luis had not been able to eliminate that terrible knot that gripped his stomach every time he cast a glance at the past: the deplorable manner in which he had broken up with his lover. He'd gotten what he'd wanted, and still he had a guilty conscience. He was finished with his messenger boy from Albion, and yet the knot was still dragging him down as if it were he, Luis, who was to blame for the fact that Stan couldn't live without him, as the young dandy had told him at the end, in tears and on his knees there in his room.

On a number of occasions during those days, both before and after moving in with the Vullionis, he visited Rafael Martínez Nadal, his lone friend in England apart from Gergorio Prieto, the famous painter from the Generation of '27. Rafael was, when you got right down to it, the only mortal he could stand at the time, but neither his words nor his friendship managed to settle him down, to sedate away his malaise and internal contradictions. There were even a couple of occasions on which Luis showed up unannounced at Rafael's house, though not to speak with him but rather to chat with his elderly mother when he knew full well that neither Rafael nor his sister Lola would be there. With the elder Nadal, he was able to release those tears which he would never have allowed himself to shed in front of Rafa, regardless of how much he loved and trusted him. On one of these occasions, he confessed to the little old lady:

"I'll always remember my father holed up in his study, obsessing over his English and Scottish tweeds. He bought the finest bolts for suits and sport coats that almost never got made. Sometimes, when I was allowed to go in and say goodnight, he was there in his study with a number of tweeds spread out on the table under the massive green crystal chandelier with the gold fringe, using a magnifying glass to scrutinize the quality and details of the textiles, testing their resistance to a sharp tug or to a flame struck by a match. It was obvious that my presence there bothered him."

These, and others like them, were the secrets that Luis allowed himself to share with his friend Rafael's mother: the rather unflatter-

ing memories of his childhood in Seville and of his parents, memories of the fountain at his house there on Calle del Tójar, where he
played with his sisters Amparo and Ana, nostalgia for his elementary
school with the priests of the Escuelas Pías order, remembrances
of that other house on Calle del Aire where they moved when his
father died. There were so many things he had tucked away in his
chest, so many things that he needed to draw out of his soul.

On this occasion, however, anchored there at the Vullioni's
home, he was yearning for the imminent hour of dawn when he
could finally tiptoe outside and introduce himself to the group of
children to whom he'd been assigned. Lying there in bed, well past
midnight, unable to fall asleep or even simply relax, he had no desire to pick up the Tolstoy novel he had been reading, and was even
less inclined to write anything. Write for what? To complain bit-
terly without resolving a single damn thing with a sense of distilled
sadness set in some beautiful nonsense verses, elegies that, in any
case, nobody would ever read? All he could do was wait for first
light to break on that frigid English spring morning so he could get
out of there and walk, bundled in his coat, down a lonely lane accompanied only by the calls of the cuckoo birds, to the farmhouse
assigned by the members of the Basque Children's Committee, the
compassionate council of philanthropic Brits who had developed
this impressive organization dedicated to educating, feeding, and
caring for the orphans of his homeland. What a shame, he thought,
growing weary during those long walks: feeding and caring for these
children from Spain simply because my fellow countrymen haven't
been able to do it themselves, being so occupied with killing one
another. And now here I am, never having wanted a child in the first
place, someone who has no idea how to talk to children or how to
understand their idiotic little world, who only likes the lithe beauty
of their bodies, their elasticity, the glossy, scented color of their skin
… but what beauty is there now in these emaciated, sickly, exposed
children? These silent little orphans with their bulging, toad-like
bellies? None. There's nothing but pity and compassion. Now, Luis
said to himself without slackening his pace down that path, I'm

stuck taking care of these kids whom I barely even know when, instead, I should have accepted the position of attaché in Oslo last fall. I'm such an idiot! What a missed opportunity! I wouldn't be here. I'd be freezing to death in Norway, but at least I'd have money in my pocket. What the hell was I thinking? My God.

Suddenly, just as he'd arrived at the sprawling farmhouse and removed his worn, winter coat, a voice jerked him from his almost trancelike state of self-absorption. It was a lanky, wispy woman, a young nurse from Almería whom he'd seen on a number of occasions; they might have even exchanged a few words during the five weeks he'd been there helping out. It was clear that the young woman had been waiting there for some time.

"There's a young boy who wants to speak with you," she said, quite suddenly and unexpectedly.

"With me?" Cernuda asked, incredulous, quite taken aback.

"Yes ... you're Luis Cernuda, right? The poet?"

"Yes," he replied, hesitant and dubious.

"The child is quite ill. He's asked to see you."

"Do I know him?"

"Perhaps, but he doesn't live in this boarding house. He stays with the older ones, the 'special' children."

He was about to ask how the child had specifically requested him, the ill-fated poet, since he didn't work at the 'special' boarding house. Did he know him? Did they know one another, the child and the homosexual? And what good would it do to ask such questions of a nurse from Almería? It's just one damn thing after another ... she wouldn't know the answer. Nobody has the answer to anything.

"What's his name?"

"José Sobrino Riaño. They call him Iñaki. If you like, I can take you to him."

"That's not necessary. Just tell me which building he lives in, and I'll go there myself."

"He's not here. They took him to the hospital in Oxford two days ago. It's best if you come with me."

"It's that serious?"

"Yes."

"Then by all means, please take me," Luis said before putting his coat back on and following the nurse out to the landing and then to the gravel driveway. A car was waiting there, the engine idling, spitting out a noxious cloud of exhaust. Once they were inside, ready to pull out, Cernuda dared to ask the one thing he didn't want to know:

"What does José have?"

"Leukemia."

Once again, the knot constricting his throat, his larynx. Worse than the knot he felt because of Richardson. It was the last straw. The height of disgrace, of disgust, of pain and human nausea. This God who does not exist, he said to himself, He's brutalizing this child … and He's not content with simply taking away his parents and snatching him from his homeland, He curses him, He poisons his blood, He abuses him with this damn childhood cancer. This is the worst of the worst, the most evil of all evils. This is the shamelessness and misery of God Himself. What does it take to appease you? he bemoaned in horrified silence.

> Pity us for once, listen to the murmuring
> Rising up like a cresting wave
> To crash at the feet of your divine indifference.
> Behold these sad stones we bear on our backs
> Ready to bury the gifts you have given us:
> The hopelessness of Beauty, Truth, and Justice,
> That you alone were able to instill in us.
> If they were to die today, you will be wiped from memory
> Like a distant dream of the men they were.

But if God does not exist, he thought to himself almost immediately, then what the fuck are you talking about, Luis? It would be deeply shameful if, after all this misery, God turned out to be real, if he actually appeared before us, cleaving the heavens in resplendent, omnipotent glory. If that was the case, he thought on the way to the hospital, he would curse Him a thousand times, for He would deserve total oblivion, our complete and utter negation, the intimate and universal human desire for Him to rot for all eternity there in his burrow, masturbating absentmindedly, ignored and fed up with the fact that nobody pays Him any attention.

22

Alfredo was passionately reading *The God Delusion* while Luis had just finished *Breaking the Spell*. Salerno Insausti had gotten there a bit early that winter morning, and was waiting for Alfredo. Luis was sitting in a large armchair, contemplative, with a strong cup of coffee in hand. Although they were different, both books said the same thing: God does not exist. He was invented by men.

"The problem is that we both already knew it," Luis said to his boyfriend when he saw him arrive there at the Barnes & Noble with his fine, thin lips and his blond hair swaying across his forehead. This time, he was wearing a tie that matched the tone of his shirt. He looked more than handsome: he looked lovely, thought Luis.

"And why is that important?"

"It's important because it's simply an ongoing onanistic act. Setting out to read something with the goal of corroborating what you already knew. It would have been better to read something that argued the complete opposite: that God exists, for example. That would have been a real challenge."

"No, Luis. Because before reading them we did not *know*, we only *thought* we knew. Now, on the other hand, we 'know' that God doesn't exist."

"But I don't 'know' for a fact," Luis replied, still with his coffee in hand. "Not having faith does not eliminate the possibility of God's existence ... objectively speaking."

"But *objectively* speaking, God doesn't exist. He only exists when you're speaking *subjectively*."

"I don't know whether God exists or not. And neither do you, nor anybody else for that matter. That's my conclusion. I don't think there's a God, but that doesn't rule out the possibility."

Tieck was on the verge of saying something, but instead chose to remain silent. A couple walked directly between the two of them: clearly they were trying to escape the cold outside. Luis sighed, gazing tenderly at his boyfriend; Alfredo was adjusting his silk tie, oblivious to the loving look.

"Furthermore," Salerno continued on that bright New York morning, "it doesn't matter in the least what I believe or know or what you believe or know. In an infinite universe, in the vastness of outer space, our beliefs don't have even the slightest bit of importance. Not even our beliefs about a God who may or not exist."

"I don't quite follow ..."

"When I say they're 'unimportant,' it implies something much more definitive, something absolute, and it's that God—when you get right down to it—is unimportant. And that's precisely what bothers me about these books, despite the enjoyment we got from reading them."

"And what is that?"

"That if God doesn't matter, then why even bother writing such judicious disquisitions explaining that God does not exist? It's as if we, all the atheists in the world, were desperate to find someone who could refute us and prove the opposite. Please, Mr. Theologian, show me where I'm wrong ... but that's just it: you'll have to be devilishly clever about it, because I'm afraid you've exhausted all your intellectual resources, and since I already know that God does not exist, it's not going to be easy to run this game on me."

"That's precisely why we read devilishly clever books that prove what we already know."

"Either I'm not understanding you, Alfredo, or you're not understanding me," Luis muttered in annoyance.

"Look, since there are no rational, scientific books capable of proving that God exists or that His existence is, at least, 'possible,' then we have no other choice but to read those other books that objectively demonstrate God's inexistence."

"Don't you see? In the end it's all just about corroborating our own obsessive objectivity, the marvels of rational methodology, and not at all about confirming or refuting God. God has been pushed into the background; all that matters is refining the scientific method, and to that end we're using God as a part of our shell game."

"But you said that God doesn't matter, Luis. That's what I don't understand."

"It doesn't matter what we believe, nor does it matter whether we die. That's what I said. In an infinite universe, these things aren't important." Here Salerno paused for a few moments; he noticed a couple at another table who were watching them intently, and finally added: "Basically it seems like a pastime for rationalists, and for that it's better to read Dostoyevsky or Sartre than to waste time doubting God, refuting or proving Him. That's what bothers me, Alfredo. It's just an unbearably vicious circle because—if I already think as Dennett and Dawkins do, and if I've already reached the same conclusion—then why the hell am I reading them?"

Tieck sat there, deep in thought, without touching his coffee, incessantly straightening his silk tie. Many years before this conversation would ever happen, in the heart of Mexico City, Jacinto had asked Luis Salerno the following question:

"And if you were ever to have a child, what would you tell him about God? Have you ever considered that?"

"First of all, let's focus on what we do, in fact, have, okay? I'm not even sure whether I want to get married. When it comes to that, at least, we're on the same page, Jacinto."

"Alright, then. But suppose you are married, a few years go by, and you have two precious little children."

"You won't face the same dilemma," Luis interrupted, smiling from ear to ear on that bright morning, sitting there in Jacinto's pied-à-terre, not far from the deafening Miguel Alemán freeway.

"Well of course not, because I'm not going to have children. Not even by mistake. I've told you that a thousand times."

Salerno remained pensive, with that broad grin still splashed across his face, as Alfredo sat lost in thought, many years later, at the Union Square Barnes & Noble. Finally, Salerno Insausti replied:

"I suppose this whole thing about faith is like the evolution of the human species, you know?" Jacinto's eyes looked like they were about to pop out of his head but he remained silent, intrigued by what he was about to hear. "Or better yet, belief in God stems from the earliest inklings of the human brain, with the first inkling of thought, and this event took place approximately 500 million years ago. And of those 500 million years, 430 million went by very slowly, uneventfully, until the point at which the first primates developed what we consider early brains. Then it would take 70 million more years for these tiny-brained primates to become what we call proto-humans. At that time, and for reasons we still don't understand, the brain would double in mass in just two million years, resulting in Homo sapiens."

"I don't know what you're trying to prove with all these fourth grade anthropological digressions."

"That faith in God surely arose and evolved on a course parallel to the human brain. That's what I'm deducing. Nothing more."

"Fine, let's assume that it did. What does that mean, Luis?"

"It means that faith in God should not be taught to and instilled in children, because nobody is ever born with that belief."

"That much we do know."

"And for precisely this reason, Jacinto: if part of the evolution of the brain itself is to one day believe in God for reason X or reason Y, and then later, to cease to believe or to continue to believe or whatever, then we should, for ethical reasons, allow children to change and evolve according to …"

"… according to their brain matter," Jacinto interrupted with a resounding laugh.

"Well, yes. You said it yourself: according to their brain matter. Why ingrain the existence or non-existence of God? What right is there to do one or the other? Why interfere with the child's natural development? To my knowledge, nobody invested a sense of faith in Homo habilis or Homo sapiens. Nobody came and taught them that God existed. Later, of course, religions were invented by a bunch of foolish, wicked crooks, but— *objectively* speaking— that has nothing to do with God. Ultimately, I believe faith arises as part of the human process, as part of the physiological and neurochemical evolution of the brain … maybe even a neuronal deficiency linked, of course, to our fear of death."

"That's all well and good, Luis. However, you know full well that there's no way to 'not teach' that God doesn't exist. It's like saying you'd rather not choose."

"So I won't teach it, pure and simple. If one of my children eventually finds God, as adults or before that or never at all, well, for better or worse, then that's it. I won't get into all that. It should be a question of simple respect to the individual with those particular neurons, and that's the child. Arguing, on the other hand, as you do, Jacinto, gets us nowhere. It's like saying I'd be to blame for the existence of a thief who robs me, because I happened to be distracted for a moment."

"Did you really say that to Jacinto?" asked Alfredo, many years later, emerging from his meditations and taking a sip of coffee.

"Yes, but for him everything that adheres to or corroborates an intuition is purely ideological, and therefore mere wordplay. Jacinto always was and continues to be Wittgensteinian, and nobody can get him out of this blind alley. Not even when I made him read Popper and his refutation of the *Tractatus* in *Open Society and Its Enemies*."

"Basically, any reasoning—any reasoned, methodical critique— is just a simple display of more or less intelligent, incisive words," Tieck said.

"Exactly," Salerno Insausti replied. "So there just came a point where there wasn't much sense in reasoning with him, since the world is, after all, a perfect piece of absurdity."

"And that's it, Luis," Jacinto had lashed out all those years ago. "Sadly enough. You have no other choice but to accept it."

"Of course it is, but that's no reason to sit here with our arms crossed and succumb to debating whether all reasoning is nothing more than simple wordplay. I just can't accept that conclusion. It would be a denial of millions of years of evolution, of criticism, of science, of progress, and reasoning. It would make me a nihilist, or worse ... There must be meaning in this world, although—as Popper says—we may never know what it is."

"There is and there isn't," Jacinto resolved, sitting cross-legged there in his living room, with a world of books at his back, reminiscent of Kien's crowded office in Canetti's *Auto-da-Fé*.

"It's always enough for you, Jacinto, when intuition coincides with reasoning, thus allowing you to argue—poorly—that everything else is an ideological or ideologized entity."

"Exactly. Everything is. We are. We can't get away from that. We're trapped in our own words, we're prisoners of our discourse, of our own bitter harangue. That's all there is to it. That's just how it is, with all due respect to you and Popper."

"But that's completely ridiculous. Looking to corroborate intuitions isn't ideological; if anything, it's psychoanalytical. For example: saying it's much better to live in Haiti than Miami simply because you can't live in Miami and are instead inevitably condemned to a life in Haiti isn't ideological. It's just an attempt at not being unhappy. It's a survival mechanism created by the brain allowing you to accept what you have, or at least acknowledge the reality of your situation. As the British say, 'That's your lot in life,' no less and no more."

"An expression which, of course, seems to me to be the height of stupidity and the supreme form of apathy," Jacinto replied.

"Or the height of joy ... look, tell me this: what other choice does the tortured prisoner have than to look at his cell through rose-colored glasses? To believe that despite it all, being there, surrounded by those four walls, isn't such a bad thing after all, provided that he's not tortured anymore? Under no circumstances is this ideological. It's sanity on the edge of the cliff, good sense in the face of vertigo. It's rationale to keep from going crazy."

"Don't you see, Luis? Don't kid yourself, it means losing your sanity, pure and simple."

"Sometimes you have to be a bit crazy to stay alive, don't you think?"

"Don't you see how the world itself is an absurdity? How we all have to roll over and play dead to keep from shooting ourselves, like Camus said?"

"That's not exactly what Camus said ..."

"Reasoning, then, according to Jacinto, would be nothing more than a means for tolerating life," Alfredo Tieck concluded, several years later, kissing Luis on the cheek. "Reasoning, for Jacinto, is a device, a simple survival trick employed by logic."

Many years before, in his pied-à-terre near the freeway, Jacinto had uncrossed his legs and responded: "Critical reasoning—the empirical method of trial and error—does not fundamentally clash with the psychological need to survive. Both are substitutes for tolerating life, for making it more bearable. We reason in order to go on living, knowing full well that, yes, the world is an absurd place, and it will be that way whether we reason or not."

23

He didn't have to wait long for a reply to appear in his inbox. Luis clicked "Enter" with an anxious heart. Who was this joker who'd written that strange, initial email?

"Sorry, my mistake. I didn't mean to write to you. It was another Luis."

Salerno Insausti was left completely petrified. He'd been hoping for anything other than this reply. Something wasn't right. He didn't believe this latest, unexpected response, this new (albeit concise) email.

He wasn't that naïve, of course; something had suddenly changed inside of this unknown person who, first, said they wanted to see his eyes again, and then said that he wasn't the intended recipient. How could they be so sure that, all of a sudden, they had the wrong person when initially they seemed quite confident and even got right to the point in asking to see his eyes? Moreover, the aforementioned yet unnamed sender hadn't even taken so much as a minute here to corroborate the mistaken identity; ergo, there had been no mistaken identity in the first place. It was him, Luis Salerno Insausti, and no other, whom this prankster had wanted to contact. This much was clear ... and if that weren't the case, why, then, the first email? Why ask to see his eyes again? And why, all of a sudden, would he or she no longer want to see them or to get in touch with him?

A bit tired of all these unanswerable questions, and frustrated by the impotence of not knowing what to do there, holed up in his apartment, Luis stood up from his swivel chair and went straight to the bathroom for a good, long piss. Pensive, he stared out the little window above the toilet at the oyster-colored full moon embroidered there above the Manhattan skyline.

24

Luis reached the hospital in Oxford feeling faint of heart. It actually seemed as if a valve had begun to atrophy; he just didn't have the strength to walk down those hallways, under the ceiling lamps. He couldn't breathe. Was it the smell of disinfectant, or was it fear? What the hell was he doing here anyway, so far away from Seville, Madrid, and Valencia, so very far away from those unforgettable gatherings at Vicente Aleixandre's house on Calle Velintonia? So far from Víctor María, Concha, Rosa, Gil-Albert, Manolo, María Teresa, Bernabé, and his other good friends from days gone by, in a damn British hospital about to speak with a child he didn't know and with whom he didn't have a damn thing in common, save for the ill-fated destiny of living in exile, speaking Spanish, and fleeing the same country awash in fratricidal turmoil? That was it; no more and no less. And yet here he was: the assistant and the one being assisted. The grown man who finds himself helping who knows how and God knows why, while the one asking for help is in truly dire straits: both trapped in a bizarre set of circumstances, compelled to converse and contemplate the situation at a foreign hospital with no other alternative but to play out their absurd, pitiful roles.

When he entered the room, the first thing that Luis saw—still half hidden by the young nurse's shoulders—were José's green eyes. Eyes that were impossible to forget: fierce and beautiful, haughty and tender, gentle and courageous. All that at once, measured and gathered, was there in that gaze. Iñaki Sobrino had a look that could see right through whatever it examined, that could discern whatever it wanted in others. Or so Cernuda thought when, stocking up on courage, he walked up to the young boy's bed feigning a steadfastness that he didn't truly feel. As soon as he laid a hand on the bed pushed up against the faded green wall, he asked:

"How are you, José?"

"Call me Iñaki, please. I don't like José. I'm Basque."

"I know," Cernuda said, as the nurse left the room, closing the door behind them. "How are you?"

"Okay," he replied in the dry, tough voice of a thirteen-year-old boy. "You? How are you?"

How should Luis respond? Really, he quickly thought to himself, what should I say? Maybe that he's not too well, but undoubtedly better than him, better than Iñaki? Tell him, perhaps, that he wasn't suffering from leukemia and that for that reason alone he should feel profoundly grateful and happy with life when in fact he wasn't, when he was actually appalled, deeply depressed, fed up with the world of men, Spaniards most of all? How should he answer the boy? In the end, he simply said:

"Good."

"You don't look good," Iñaki replied. "You look bad."

Shit. I look bad, and yet he's the one lying there, dying, in a hospital bed?

"Really?" was the only thing he could think of to say. Immediately he chose to change the subject and said, "They said you asked for me."

"Yes. We've already met ... I mean ..." Iñaki hesitated. "I met you before they sent me to the new boarding house. You know, the 'special' one."

"I'm sorry, I don't remember."

"That's okay. It doesn't matter. I was always with my brother Luis. He's three years younger than me."

"Oh, really?"

"One time you went up to Luis and said that you both had the same name, and then you talked for a while. My brother told you that he'd written some poetry for my mother, remember? I was there, but it doesn't matter you don't remember me. My name's not Luis, and I'm not a poet like you."

"And how do you know that I'm a poet?"

"You told my brother that same day."

"That's right," he lied, not remembering the encounter. So many things had happened during the past five weeks; he'd met so many children.

"It was about a month ago, or a little less."

"Right around the time I arrived."

"I guess."

"I haven't been around that long, you know?"

"We haven't either."

"You came with the rest of the kids. On board *El Habana.*"

"Yes. We thought we'd just be here for a few weeks. We haven't seen our mother since then. We haven't heard anything about her. We don't even know if she's alive or not."

"And your dad?"

"My dad died at the front, during the siege. I was with him ..." He paused for a moment, not sure whether to continue. "He died right next to me. He was holding me in his arms. We were both in the trench that I helped to dig, along with one of my uncles. He kissed me, or tried to kiss me, and then he died. A bullet hit him right in the neck and he bled out very quickly. That's all I remember: my dad bleeding. He didn't even say anything to me. He couldn't; his mouth was so full of blood. All he could do was squeeze me so hard that he left marks on my skin. Marks that I still have ... look. Every time I see these marks, it reminds me of him. He was really nice to Luis and me. We loved him a lot. It sounds strange to say we loved him, you know? I feel like I still do love him even though he's not here. Even though he's dead. When I want to remember him, I touch the marks he left on me on that day."

"I'm sorry," Luis gasped. What else was there to say? What else could he have said, even if he had breath enough with which to say it? One more story amongst the thousands of other, similar stories, some worse than others, some better, and his, the story of Luis Cernuda, to this day, at thirty-six years of age, past the midpoint of life ... was it one of the worst? Or somewhat less bad? Perhaps it could even be the best of all, he thought dejectedly, sardonically. Who knows ...

"So why did they move you to a 'special' boarding house?"

"You don't know?"

"No."

"The older ones, the ones who fought in the war … they decided to send us to other locations. They called us 'the difficult boys,'" he said with a halfhearted laugh.

"Yes, I've heard about 'the difficult boys,' but I believe you're the first I've met."

"Supposedly they're more lenient with us, more relaxed. They let us do more and sleep later, but I wasn't like that. In the beginning, and because I was learning English so quickly, Lord Farringdon thought of sending me to a private school, but I didn't want to go."

"Why?"

"I don't know," he said hesitantly. "For lots of reasons. I thought we'd be sent back to Spain soon, I didn't want to be away from my brother, I wasn't interested in school …"

"What were you interested in?"

"Getting better. Getting strong enough to go back to Spain. And killing them. Killing everyone who murdered my father and my uncles."

Cernuda fell silent. He waited for a moment or two, indecisive. Finally, he asked Iñaki, whose voice was beginning to fade noticeably:

"And your brother? Where is he?"

"I asked for him to be here with me when they transferred me, and he has been here the entire time. He just left a couple of hours ago. I'll see him tomorrow, I guess. I don't seem to be doing too well, but they don't tell me anything. They don't want to."

"You look a little tired."

"I am."

"Do you want me to go?"

"Yes, but could you come back tomorrow?"

"Of course," Cernuda replied, desperate to get out of there, to escape, on the verge of breaking down and crying, of kicking the walls, or just screaming.

"Promise?" Iñaki insisted as he rolled over in bed, his back to Luis, his eyelids getting heavy.

"I promise. I'll talk with the nurse."

"And please read some of your poems to me. I would love to hear them."

Without hugging him, without kissing him, without even touching him, Cernuda left the room like a sleepwalker. For a moment, he envied Federico's fate: his best friend no longer had to endure any of this.

25

Ever since childhood, as far back as he could remember, he'd always sought out what doesn't change, he'd longed for eternity. Everything around him contributed, in his early years, to sustaining the illusion and the belief that it would last: the unchanging family home, the accidents that defined of his life. If anything changed, it was only to return later to its usual state, everything proceeding like the year's cycle of seasons, and behind the apparent change an intimate unity always shone through.

But childhood ended and he tumbled into the world. People around him died and houses fell into ruin. As he was then possessed by the delirium of love, he didn't pay any attention to this evidence of human decay. If he had discovered eternity's secret, if he possessed eternity in spirit, what did the rest matter? But no sooner had he pressed a body close to his, believing his desire was imbuing it with permanence, than it fled his arms, leaving them desolate.

Later he loved animals, trees (He'd loved a black poplar, a white poplar), the earth. Everything disappeared, planting in his solitude the bitter feeling of the ephemeral. He alone seemed to last amid the transience of things. And then, cruelly certain, the notion of his own eventual disappearance dawned on him, the sense that he too one day would abandon his self.

God, he'd said then, give me eternity! God for him was still the love not attainable in this world, the love forever unbroken, triumphant over the double-edged trick of time and death. And he loved God like the perfect and incomparable friend.

It was just another dream, because God does not exist. The dry leaf, crushed in passing, told him so. The dead bird told him, its broken wing rotting on the ground. Consciousness told him, knowing it too would be lost one day in the vastness of nonbeing. And if God doesn't exist, how could he?

26

Bored, driven by the inertia of his nocturnal idleness, Luis clicked his inbox for the umpteenth time. An email from Augusto. He opened it:

"José's not good. Going to the hospital. Call you later."

No sooner had he finished reading this single line from his dear brother-in-law than his cell phone rang, sending an electric shock up his spine for a millisecond: a synthetic, cellular premonition.

With no small amount of effort, and still reeling from the news, he reached for the device and immediately heard:

"Hi Luis. It's Diana. Please don't hang up. I just called to tell you that your nephew José is really sick. They took him to the emergency room ..."

"Wait, what? I just wrote to Marcela. She didn't mention anything."

"It all happened really fast. That's why I'm calling. He woke up feeling really bad, and got worse as the day went on. They just took him to the ER an hour ago ... It seems complicated. The doctors are trying everything."

"What does that mean?" Luis shouted as he stood up, as if that simple act could somehow change anything. "What does he have? How do they not know what to do?"

"They don't know. He can barely breathe, and he's turning blue all the time. I'm here at the hospital, Luis. He's making these scary noises, like an old man snoring. Like a death rattle ..."

"Bronchitis?"

"No, no," Diana said, raising her voice. "Something much worse. It seems like a virus has lodged in his heart. It's serious, Luis. Really very serious. Marcela and Augusto are terrified. They can't stop crying."

"Could I talk with Marcela?"

"She can't. She's in the operating room. I have to go. I promise I'll call you later. Adiós."

Diana hung up the phone. Luis wanted to add something, to ask another question, to find out everything, as if doing so would somehow cure his nephew's illness, or at least postpone the inevitable. He was shivering, breaking into a cold sweat; just then, a couple of tears rolled down his cheek. He didn't know why. He didn't know José, Marcela's youngest child, and again—after that realization and without his consent—more tears began to flow. It was as if Marcela herself were sick, and he was not at her side. As if she were five years old and he was eight or nine and here he was, far away, full of fear, powerless to stop the hacking cough plaguing the sister he loved as much as he loved himself. Marcela was José and José was Marcela and it was the same, strange pain: perhaps a nervure or fissure in the cerebellum that suddenly sends out a jolt of vibrations and makes you feel fucking awful, yes, really fucking awful. That's what the pain was like.

He got a small suitcase, the first one he saw when he reached under his unmade bed, grabbed his passport and the first three shirts in his dresser, turned out the lights, and double bolted the door. He flew down the five floors of his building and burst out into the busy, noisy street. And before he got in the first cab he hailed, he caught a glimpse of the same, oyster-colored moon bathing the night, though nobody in all of Manhattan even noticed it.

27

Before confronting his father, Luis Salerno had met with his half sister in a café. It was a Sunday: he'd returned from Monterrey on Saturday night, and not on Tuesday as he had planned. In the end, he didn't go with Diana to McAllen after that whole barrage of truths and mutual insults that had erupted at his cousin Adriana's house. Maybe, he thought, it would have been better not to talk to Diana, let alone confront her, but it was too late for that now. In any case, Luis didn't feel that he was to blame: it was all because of Diana, because of *that* inexplicable thing which he self-assuredly referred to as a "despicable act of collusion" between his father and his sister, something too disgraceful, too appalling to be either understood or forgiven.

He and Amparo spent the first three hours there at the little bistro Luis had selected, not far from his apartment. Then, neither tired nor eager to leave, they spent a few more hours back at his place, alone, ruminating over their respective lives, reviewing them, comparing them, breaking them down. They both wanted to get into to the minutiae of the story, to the watermark on the page on which the story had been written, if such a thing were even possible.

The more he looked at his half sister, the more Luis felt he was looking at a portrait of his father. A female portrait, true, but in the end there was a striking similarity between the two: the jaw line, the oval shape of the head, the teeth, the small mouth, the large ears ... even her hands resembled those of his father. It was like a womanly version of his precursor, albeit twenty years younger.

"So," Luis asked, lighting his fifth cigarette of the day, "how old was your mother when she met my dad?"

"She said she was twenty-three and your dad was twenty-two."

"So your mother is older ..." Luis was about to add 'than my dad,' but he stopped short: saying 'my dad' instead of 'our dad' could be ambiguous, although perhaps somewhat partisan. But saying 'our dad' felt rather strange, and could even come across as excessive to his new half sister. He wasn't quite sure, he couldn't hazard a guess as to how this new human being—so close to him and yet still so far away—might react. How should he handle this? What words should he select for this conversation? Should he consider each and every one of them? Why not just talk, say what he wanted to say, speak his mind as the thoughts arrived?

Amparo was beautiful. Chatty, talkative, and effusive, unlike him. He appreciated this; she seemed like a decent person. She was who she was. It was obvious that she didn't care what other people might think of her, but at the same time Luis was able to intuit that behind his half sister's words there lay a sense of fear, one that was hard to define even for her. It was as if Amparo had to fill every little cranny of silence with voices, with sentences, with gestures, never falling silent at the risk of being exposed, of discovering something unwonted about herself, something uncertain that she was afraid to find. Luis, however, didn't feel that this verbal wall had anything to do with him or with anyone in general; no, that wall protected her from herself, from something very personal (and arcane) that she didn't know and didn't want to know. Still, though, Luis pretended that he wasn't aware of all that, as if his ability to break through those exterior walls were limited, and instead was quite happy and content with what she was willing to offer up to him.

"My mother said, first, that she was pregnant, and he told her that he would call her later, that they should take some time and think calmly about what was best to do." Amparo said.

"That's not exactly true, Luis," his father told him two days later. "I just wasn't sure that the child was mine."

"What are you talking about? Why, Dad?"

"I can't tell you that, Luis, without hurting her, and the last thing I ever wanted to do, since this girl came into my life, was to hurt her …"

"But that girl is your daughter, Dad …" Luis countered, lighting a cigarette. "You can tell me," he insisted. "It's not going to hurt me, Dad. I promise you."

"Amparo's mother wasn't just sleeping with me. Around that

same time, she was also sleeping with one of my best friends, Guillermo."

"I can't believe it," Luis said, dumbstruck, sucking on his cigarette without looking his father in the face. Of all the possible outcomes, this was the one he least expected.

"Let's just say that her mother was a woman of easy virtue. You understand me, Luis," his father emphasized, as if he hadn't been sufficiently explicit. "Two months later, I sat down with her father."

"You met with her father?"

"Yes, and it wasn't just me ... Guillermo was there too. We both went to see him when he called me into his office on Reforma. There was, however, no need to get into details. Thank God I was spared that unpleasantness. He simply told me that his daughter was pregnant and that I didn't have to worry about a thing, that they knew how to deal with the situation, and after that I never heard from her again. I didn't know if she had the baby or if she got an abortion. I didn't know anything, Luis, and neither Guillermo nor I wanted to find out. It was a clean break. But one thing I will tell you is this: there's just as much of a chance that she's his daughter as there is of her being mine. You see?"

"Your grandfather," his aunt Adriana — his father's older sister — confessed to him a week later when he called her to ask if she knew anything about Amparo, "told him just to wash his hands of the situation, that there was nothing for him to do. Your father, Luis, was very young and inexperienced. Your grandfather didn't want to see your father's future cut short, right when it seemed as if he had everything to look forward to. Your grandfather was very old-fashioned. He believed that such mistakes were the woman's fault, and that the man had nothing to do with it."

"And what kind of a man was my grandfather?" Luis thundered.

"Don't be angry. Those were different times back then," aunt Adriana said, from the other end of the line.

"Go and meet with the man at his office, like he asked. Take Guillermo with you, and whatever he asks, just tell the truth. Tell him you weren't the only one, that his daughter was sleeping with both of you. There's no way around it. It's going to hurt deep down in his guts, but I'm not about to let my only son's life be ruined because of some girl who doesn't know how to take care of herself and, on top of that, who goes around sleeping with more than one guy at a time."

"But I've seen her, Dad. She looks just like you," Luis insisted. "She's yours. She's your daughter. I'm sure of it."

"It's all relative," his father cut him off sharply on that morning, two days later. "Do you know my friend Guillermo?"

"I met him when I was little, but I don't remember much. It's been years since you've seen each other, right?"

"He's blonde like she is, and Guillermo looks a lot like me. Don't you see? Amparo could just as easily be his daughter. She has his features."

"And why can't she be your daughter? Tell me that. To me, it looks like Amparo has your features, Dad, and to take it one step further, Amparo looks more like you than my own sister Diana does. Life is ironic like that …"

"That's enough, Luis. It's like you're attacking me. I don't know what you want. I don't know where you're going with this investigation. Are you on her side, or mine?"

"I'm not on anybody's side. I'm on the side of truth, of what's fair, of what should have been done four decades ago but wasn't. No, I don't agree with what you or your friend Guillermo failed to do, what you left out. I can't stand this culture of deception. We have to seek the truth, whatever the cost, Dad, even though we may never find it …"

"And what truth is that, Luis? You'd be the last one to understand that. After all, nobody invited you to this party."

"Excuse me, but yes, this *is* my party. Of *course* it's my party." Luis was on the verge of raising his voice, and the ash on the end of his cigarette was growing. "From the moment you had a daughter, it didn't matter with whom or when or where … she automatically became my sister, so yes, that makes it *my* party, pure and simple. Understand? That's how it is. That's what I believe. In fact, Diana and Marcela and even you, Dad, are invited to this party as well. I'm not going to turn away from Amparo as easily as Diana did just because you cried and begged her. She's your daughter. Yes, your biological daughter, and that means something. It means a lot. It means everything."

"You know, my mother says that it was a rather large group of friends," Amparo said, getting up from the table to serve some coffee. Now the two of them were at Luis's apartment, not far from the café where they had met. They had been talking for over five hours that afternoon, which was about to turn into an evening downpour there in Mexico City. "They got together almost every weekend to do something: get dinner, go dancing, smoke some weed, catch a rock band, or even a little getaway to Taxco, Tajimara, Veracruz, Puebla, Cuernavaca ..."

"The first time I slept with her," their father said, "was in Las Estacas. We slipped away from the group and we did it. The second and final time was when we were already back in Mexico City. Things just weren't going to work; we both knew it, we knew it immediately after it happened. There was no need to push or prolong the thing, you know? A simple matter of bad chemistry. Later I learned that Amparo's mother had slept with Guillermo around that same time too. To be clear: she wasn't my girlfriend or anything like that. I had no right to demand anything of her. But to go from there to being the father of her future child ... that's quite a leap, Luis."

"*My dad* was young," Amparo said, referring to Luis's father as her own for the first time. Salerno Insausti was amazed by the word with which Amparo chose to use *for their father* after only having met Luis a little over five hours ago, and without once having heard her say "my father." It was all so strange, so confusing. Now Amparo was justifying him ... or trying to, to some degree. At least, that's what Luis felt at the time. Better yet, it was as if Amparo wanted to justify their father's actions in order to feel a little less badly about him, in order to be able to better understand the inexplicable: the things that happen when we're not around to witness them, before we ever existed, when we're yet to be born, when we were nothing but a fetus or whatever it is that happens in the universe when a man's sperm merges with a woman's egg by some randomness of the world. It was all so strange, so absurd.

"So you've seen him, Amparo?" asked Luis.

"Of course. Several times. It took me a while to decide whether to go look for him the first time. I didn't think I could do it, but I did. I went to see him."

"And ... ?"

"You know what? Deep down I don't think he cared much or was very interested or knew what the hell to do with me, with my existence, with this daughter of his who suddenly popped up out of nowhere when he already had grown children. He didn't want to even think about dealing with anything that had to do with the past."

"I don't know what this kid wants from me," her father said to Luis two days later on that lengthy, rainy reunion. "I've seen her, we've talked a few times, and I still have no idea what she wants me to do, now that more than forty years have gone by."

"And what do you want, Amparo?" Luis asked. "What would you like to have happen?"

"I'd like to have a dad," she said, confident and self-assured, as if she had been answering that question since she was ten years old. "I've always wanted to have a dad. But I never did. No brothers, either."

"And your step father?"

"I guess you'd say he's my mother's husband," she replied with a smile. "But he's not my dad. He's a great guy, but he didn't come into my life until I was already fourteen. He was never really my dad."

"So what happened? What was it like growing up?"

"My mom told me that I didn't have a father. That's how I lived my entire life until one day I got fed up with all the excuses and told my mother that couldn't be true. My dad must have had a name, and I wanted to know what it was. Finally, after a year of persistence, my mom finally told me, and that's when I realized that my supposedly deceased father wasn't actually dead."

"I don't understand, Amparo."

"My mom had always said that my dad had died, and that was it. End of discussion. She never mentioned his name. But eventually I found out. I learned who he was, I learned everything about him, despite the fact that my mother forbid it. She was trying to talk me out of doing it, from getting in touch with him. It's like she already knew, like she was anticipating all the bad stuff that's happened to me since then: his cold detachment, his lack of interest, his complete sense of disdain. A less stubborn person would have let all this rest in peace, Luis, I know, but not me. I always wanted a dad, and I wasn't about to give up."

"You know, son, I asked her once, 'Why do you want to have a father, Amparo?' And guess what … she had no idea how to respond. All she could say was that she wanted a dad and that her mom had assured her that I was the one. Even though she's a grown woman, married, with kids. Her life was complete. So why be so stubborn with me then? Why does she all of a sudden want me to be her dad? Frankly, I just don't get it. I don't know how to deal with all of this. That's why I asked Diana not to reveal all this in the first place. I mean, what's the point?"

"There are things, Dad," Luis said, still clutching his cigarette, brandishing it as if it were a double-edged sword. "Things we can't or shouldn't understand. Things get done and that's it. They're done for justice. If she wants you to be her father (which, in fact, you are), then what the hell is the harm in that? I don't understand. It's only fair. It's all she's asking for."

"But nobody really knows who her father is. And let me tell you this: as far as I'm concerned, it's Guillermo. I've always believed that, just as much as he's refused to acknowledge it."

"Dad, the reason he wouldn't acknowledge it is because Amparo's mother knew that you—not him, but you—were her daughter's father. It's not about your friend wanting anything to do with her or not. It's about the simple fact that Guillermo doesn't have a dog in this fight, and that for forty years you've been using that excuse to justify your actions, to defend yourself."

"The last time I spoke with dad," Amparo said, this time without her possessive pronoun, "I asked him for a DNA test. I never wanted it to get to that point, but he just kept stonewalling me. So in a flood of tears, riddled with doubt, I asked him. You can't even imagine what it was like, Luis. It took me two whole weeks to work up the courage to do it."

"She was bawling, Luis, and I had no idea how to console her. I'd told her time after time that if what she wanted was a father, then she could call me that."

"This one time," Amparo exclaimed, almost angrily, splashing a few drops of coffee on the wooden table, "he said that if what I wanted was a father ... then he'd be that for me, that he'd gladly fulfill that need. It was offensive, I have to admit. I'm not sure why. It felt like he was trying to sugarcoat everything, that he was just giving me the cold shoulder until I stopped bothering him. Does that make sense?"

"And then, on another occasion—you're not gonna believe this—she asked me for a DNA test, and I said why the hell would you want that, after I already agreed to be the one thing you wanted most: a father. Yes, her father. Amparo can be pretty stubborn. Really."

"Now you're just dodging the issue," Amparo had said on that distant occasion. She was speaking casually with him, less formal, the way she did when they were alone at a downtown café. "If you are, the DNA will prove it, and if you're not, it'll confirm that too. There's nothing to lose and a lot to gain. Don't you see?"

"But Amparo, you yourself told me that what you wanted most in the world was a father, and I already told you that, yes, I'll be your dad if you want," Luis's father had insisted. "I don't understand ... what more do you want?"

"No, not like that. I don't want anyone forced into being my father. I want you or whomever it is to really, truly want to be my father. And you don't. That's clear as day. I don't matter to you. You hate me."

"Of course I don't hate you."

"Tell me one thing, Dad . . ." Luis had said that afternoon, finally relighting the cigarette that had been sitting there on the silver ashtray. "Let's just assume that Amparo's mother is lying when she says that you're the only one who could be her true father. Why would she do that? Why has she never once mentioned Guillermo?"

"How could I possibly know that?" he countered, his voice rising as he felt himself being cornered.

"Just tell me why a mother would lie to her own daughter?" Luis fired back, though for a clear yet fleeting moment he realized that this question could ultimately be posed to himself. "Why lie, why deceive her when you've already postponed the moment of truth for twenty long years, and now your daughter is asking you, she's hounding you, and she deserves to know? It doesn't make sense, Dad. If this woman didn't know anything, she wouldn't have said anything. That's what I think. No mother would be capable of falsifying something so serious, and with such consequences. If you're not sure, you don't speak up. But if Amparo's mother says you're her father, then you're her father, like it or not." Luis was relentless, unstoppable, and confident in his argument.

"In the end, he didn't want to take the DNA test. He didn't refuse it, Luis; he just kept putting it off. He said he'd call me, but he didn't. I called him and he swore he'd call me back. And that was the last time we met. I'm disappointed . . . I'm just so disappointed in him. What kind of a man is my dad?" There it was again — *my dad* — and Luis felt the hairs on his arm stand on end.

"If you refused to take a DNA test," Luis had said with the utmost assurance on that day, which was the last time he saw his father before leaving for New York just a couple of months later, "then it can only mean one thing: deep down in your heart, you know full well that, yes, you are Amparo's father and despite that fact you've been trying all this time to mislead her without much success. You've decided to live in your own little world of ambivalence, you've chosen to base your life on your hollow premise, citing your belief that — despite all the evidence to the contrary — she's not yours, that instead she's your old friend Guillermo's daughter." Here he paused to collect himself before adding, "Look, I understand, like aunt Adriana says, grandpa would have recommended that you not to get involved in all this, even though you should have taken some action forty years ago, Dad. I understand that. You were just a fresh-faced kid, you were scared shitless, and you had no idea what to do with a young, pregnant girl. That thing I don't understand, and which I can't forgive, is the way you're treating Amparo today. She's your own daughter. Not only has she had to suffer the lack of a father her whole damn life, but now, to make matters worse, she has to suffer your scorn, your cowardice."

"Don't you take that tone with me, Luis. I forbid it."

"You can't stop me from doing anything," Luis countered, undaunted on the last occasion that they would see one another. "Because after today, you'll never see me again. But first there's something you should know, something you should understand loud and clear, Dad: Amparo won't be your daughter if you don't want her, but she is my sister, and I was incredibly happy to have found that out thanks to Jacinto running his mouth off, believe it or not. Diana, on the other hand, though she would never admit it, is cut from the same cloth as you. You're exactly alike. You signed on to this depraved conspiracy of silence with her. That much is clear. You wanted to keep this from Marcela and me, because you knew that neither of us were going to stand for it. But thank you, though, for Amparo. Really. You took Diana away from me, but you replaced her for me with someone so much better. Thanks."

28

"The thing is that all of us are going to die. Some later than others … Ultimately, death is an endless chain. It's neither good nor evil. It just comes for us."

"That's just a bunch of platitudes, Luis."

"That might be true, but it's still worth taking into consideration." Salerno Insausti stopped here, and — after a short pause — he asked Alfredo on that particular morning: "You, for example … do you believe your death is set for a particular date?"

"I don't understand," Tieck declared, almost angry at the absurd turn this conversation had taken since he'd arrived at his boyfriend's apartment with the promise of having a decent cup of espresso … which, by the way, still hadn't happened. The lack of coffee was making him nervous. "Set by who?"

"No one. Just set," Luis replied emphatically before lighting a cigarette. "My mother thinks there's a day for everyone. A specific day."

"Of course everyone has his day. You can't have two. You can't die on two different days, Luis," Alfredo chuckled. He fully understood the intent of the question, of course, but chose instead to avoid it. All he wanted was his coffee, and maybe a toasted bagel with cream cheese. That was all, and then, perhaps, some morning lovemaking with his Mexican boyfriend.

"I'm not joking around, Alfredo. I'm wondering about a particular date, an exact date, one day out of all the days of the year when we are set to die, regardless of what we do or fail to do, just like that story *The Arabian Nights*. Does such a specific moment exist?"

"Is the day of our death preordained?" Alfredo clarified without knowing how the hell to respond, or where his boyfriend was going with all this.

"Yes," Luis confirmed. "Not so much preordained, but at least a day that's been set, the difference being that we, as mortals, of course, don't know when this day might be. A day which — though we don't know it, owing to certain innate limitations—already exists. That's what my mother believes. You see?"

"I just can't believe in anything that claims to be prophetic or oracular. Don't forget about all the dire consequences involved when you employ arguments based on a nonexistent future. All the genocides that were committed under the sophism of a future filled with light, because of the false promise of a marvelous future. Nothing like that exists. An argument based on the future is a lie. When it exists, it'll happen. Not before. In that sense, our own death does not exist, nor has it ever existed. And it won't until it actually happens."

"So death doesn't live within us? It isn't nestled in our hearts? Isn't death somehow a part of life?"

"That death gives meaning to life is a completely different matter. And yes, that's something I can understand," Alfredo Tieck said, "but to go from there to thinking that my death is predetermined and that I don't know the date ... well, that's something I can't believe."

"I'm not saying I believe it, Alfredo. All I'm saying is that I've been asking myself that question all night long," Salerno Insausti said, downcast, pensive, motionless, sucking on his cigarette with serious intent only to release a lungful of smoke. "To a certain extent, it's easy to respond the way you do: rationally. You should realize that—at least when it comes to death—I would have to think differently, or at least try to. When you get down to it," he said, without emerging from his apathetic or melancholic state, "it's easier to be rational, to give a rational explanation, than to admit the possibility of irrationality when it comes to death. In this case, it's irrational to believe that—unbeknownst to us—our death may well have been prearranged since birth. I know it sounds absurd, Alfredo, but it's only absurd because it's irrational."

"In other words, you realize that if you're thinking like your mother, you won't be able to make heads nor tails of anything."

"Rationally, yes. I realize that."

"But nevertheless, at the same time, you're trying to say that if, for example, if we were to abstain from using reason, then we could speculate about our day being predestined. Is that it?"

"Yeah, more or less," Luis said, glancing out the window for a moment, almost ashamed of his agonizing irrationalism.

The two of them fell silent for a few seconds. Alfredo was pensive while Salerno Insausti sank back into the warmth of his sorrow on that New York morning. After a brief pause, Tieck picked up the threads of their unfinished conversation.

"Why did my father die on June 15th, when I was nine? Tell me. Why didn't he die when I was twenty or thirty? Is that it, Luis? Is that the question? Why do things happen on one day and not on another? What's significant about dying on that date as opposed to any other? What the hell can you possibly pin on the date of someone's death? Is there something arcane or mysterious that goes above and beyond our pathetic understanding?"

"I guess that's the question, yeah."

"No, it's not, Luis. That's *not* the issue. Nothing symbolizes anything," Alfredo said in an almost angry burst. "We just want to bestow symbols and significance on empty events. There's no meaning in dying on a particular day other than what you give it. There is no actual significance in dying. Things happen and that's it. We are, however, stupidly programmed to try to unravel mysteries that aren't really there. Dying on this day or that doesn't symbolize a damn thing, Luis. Believe me."

"But was it determined to be that way?" Salerno Insausti lashed out, still not quite satisfied, resisting the harsh, pristine reality being demonstrated by his boyfriend.

"The problem is that when you use words like 'determined' or 'set,' the question that inevitably arises is, who set it up that way? Who made the determination?"

"Nobody, Alfredo. That's the thing."

"Don't you see? A decision can't be made by Nobody. It's ontological and even grammatical nonsense. Unless, of course, you say it's God who makes the call, but you've always said you don't believe in God."

"I don't, but I'm open to the possibility that there's Something absurd or irrational tucked away here in this world."

"If you admit that, then you're also admitting the possibility that there is Someone who determines the future, an Architect who knows the course of events over time."

"But let me say it again, Alfredo: I don't believe in God."

"By thinking that death is forecast, determined, preordained or whatever, then deep down, you're presuming that Someone or Something has planned it all out ahead of time," Tieck insisted. "And that's exactly what your beloved Popper is attacking when it comes to the future of humanity, which—if you remember—doesn't exist. You explained it to me yourself." Alfredo paused here to catch his breath before adding, in a sudden, mystical fit: "Death is always conjugated in the present."

Luis was about to say something, but instead remained silent. So Tieck then continued: "And believe me, it doesn't symbolize anything."

"My nanny died yesterday, Alfredo," Salerno suddenly blurted out.

"Say what?"

"She fell off the roof and died. They say it was instantaneous, that she didn't suffer, though they don't know for sure. My mother called me last night to tell me. I couldn't stop crying."

"I'm so sorry." Alfredo replied, not knowing what to say. Who was this Mexican nanny? "Were you very close with her?"

"She looked after me. I played with her whenever my parents went out to a party or to go see a movie. She really loved me, and I loved her too. She never had children of her own. She was such a good woman ... so extremely sweet and patient with my sisters and me."

"Did she live with your parents?"

"For many years, yes. And that seems like the worst part about it, doesn't it? So much younger than both of them, and yet she was the first to go. My sisters and I always thought—though we never dared to say it—that she would be the one to take care of them when they got older."

"So that's why you want to know what her death means? That's why you're wondering whether it was prophesized in some way?" Alfredo asked, getting up from his armchair and going over to Luis to give him a gentle hug, patting his shoulder and stroking his tousled hair. "I'm so sorry. I just had no idea why the hell all you wanted to talk about this morning was death. You could have told me right when I got here."

"I wanted to get the truth straight from your heart, Alfredo. I wanted to hear the harsh reality, which of course — deep down — I already knew." As he said this, he almost wanted to laugh in spite of his pain. "You just confirmed what I already knew. Her untimely death means nothing, and neither does mine or yours. No one can prophesize or forecast death ... whether it's early or late or tragic or medical."

"Not even a powerful dictator or king could prophesize my death, and do you know why? Because the future doesn't exist. We can force it, we can compel it, but the future, such as it is, simply does not exist."

Alfredo didn't know what more he could say, what the hell he could possibly add to this theory. He was confused and trembling, and not just by the news but also by his cold, implacable rationalism. He hesitated for a few seconds. Then, finally, hoping to break through the thin layer of ice, he asked his boyfriend:

"And your mother, how is she?"

"She and my father spent all afternoon yesterday at the police department and now they have the funeral coming up. My nanny's parents are still alive. They're very poor, and she has teenage siblings, can you believe it? My mother told me it was written. She believes that her death was always going to happen yesterday."

"She felt it?"

"No, not like that. She believed it after the fact."

"Your mother talks like that because she believes in God. It's comforting for her to think like that, to feel that — despite it all — it wasn't in her power to save her."

"But she says she doesn't believe in God."

"That's what she claims, but deep down she believes all things have a transcendent, metaphysical purpose, something distant and unknown to us, the mere mortals. When we believe in the Great Beyond, it's a lot easier to believe in the absurd notion that death occurs because of some enigmatic reason."

"Harsh reality," said Luis.

"Death isn't harsh; it's nothing at all ... and you know what? For me, it's reassuring to know that there's no hereafter," Luis's Chilean boyfriend said, and then—still holding his hand—he added: "Do you want to go to Mexico?"

"It wouldn't make any sense, Alfredo. My sisters are going to the burial, and you know I don't want to see my father. Now all I've got is my stomach tied up in knots over all this. I can't cry. I couldn't sleep last night. All I could do was think about her, remembering the games she made up for us to play when we were kids, the afternoons my sisters and I spent with Rosi running around in the yard, the songs from her town that she taught us, the pranks we pulled on her ... I even remembered the warnings and punishments she doled out when we misbehaved or disobeyed her."

"You'll be able to cry," Tieck said, still holding his hand, having completely forgotten about his espresso and his toasted bagel with cream cheese.

"That's why, when you first got here, I told you that death is like a chain, and it almost seems as if there's a date printed on each and every link."

"Yes, death is like a chain, as you said, but nothing is written on any of the links, Luis. Absolutely nothing."

Nevertheless, that would be the next to last time that he would hear Alfredo's soft, firm voice, because four or five days later, Salerno Insausti would catch him in a Soho bar kissing another young man. He didn't want to find out if this was just some passing fling, some insignificant slipup, if he'd taken the time to get to know this new man (and betray him, Luis), if he was in love with one of them or both (him and this unknown man), since all these love affairs end up spiraling out of control. None of that mattered much at that point: Alfredo Tieck, his first same-sex love, his best friend in New

York, had simply died, because something inside of him (something ineffable) had died as well. The same dull, blunt, austere pain he felt upon learning of his nanny's death came back to him that night in Soho when he caught Alfredo cheating. Shortly afterwards, all that was left was a phone call and a few tears. No shouting, no complaining, no protesting. In the end, their passion, their love story, ended with a short, simple, insincere *See you later*. Luis never remembered the details of that last conversation with Tieck, but he did, however, recall quite clearly the other conversation they had on the day Rosi, his nanny, died in Mexico.

Either way, a fair amount of time had passed since that particular occasion.

29

That same night, after having visited Iñaki at the hospital, Luis was taken back to the Vullioni's house. Quite frankly, he felt as if he were grieving. He didn't want to see anyone and luckily for him, that's how it turned out. When he opened the door and removed his overcoat, the owners of the home were nowhere to be found, which meant he didn't have to greet them or exchange any pleasantries in English, so after hanging up his scarf and umbrella, he was able to steal away into his room, which was just across the hall from theirs. As soon as the door swung shut behind him, he took off his jacket and undid his tie. With no small amount of effort, he removed his shoes, and immediately collapsed into bed. Only then did he realize that he hadn't eaten so much as a bite all day, though he still didn't have much of an appetite. On the contrary, he felt a pain in the pit of his stomach, a burning right there in his gut. Might he have gastritis? But not even that concern was more disturbing than his memory of José Sobrino, the image of his green eyes and his angular face, his pale temples, his thin, damp hair, his emaciated body lying there on the meager hospital bed, just as meager as his, with the difference being that Iñaki's frail body was lying there like a lifeless eel, his slight little frame turning purple, livid, sick with leukemia. Even thinking about that word—leukemia—left him a little choked up every time it crossed his mind; he hadn't been able to get it out of his head ever since he'd left the hospital. The word was flashing through his head like a bolt. Involuntarily, he associated it with another word: poison. Yes, he'd heard it many times before, though he didn't know if it was true, that leukemia was nothing but pure poison in the blood, a kind of poison in the red and white blood cells. Of course, it had to be more than that, something much, much worse, but in his mind, all Luis could picture was a sort of liquid venom, like rat or cockroach poison circulating though the blue veins of the little Basque boy. Laid out in bed, Luis impassively contemplated the faint lapis lazuli stains on the ceiling of his borrowed room. He had to stop thinking about Iñaki; there was nothing to be gained from delving into someone else's pain because there was nothing he could do about it, nothing aside from tormenting himself in vain. Damn it all. Why had he taken this job? What the hell was Stanley thinking? How was sending him to Oxfordshire helping him in any way? Why hadn't he accepted the job in Oslo when he'd had the chance? Why hadn't he just stayed in Paris? Why? Just ... why? Clearly, it would be better to try to read something to distract himself; he needed to stop thinking about Iñaki and all those other sad, unanswerable questions that had been left behind, discarded like all the other things that hadn't happened in his life.

He decided to try to continue on with *Anna Karenina*. Reluctantly, he picked up his copy of the book and opened it. He'd already read the first half of it in French. One of his good friends, the writer Rosa Chacel, had given it to him when he'd first visited Paris the year before, and while before he could get carried away and read like a madman, once he accepted the ill-fated job of working with exiled children, he hadn't been able to get back into it. But now was his chance to do exactly that. He removed the bookmark and began to read from chapter seven of part four, where Stepan Arkadyevich Oblonsky returns from abroad to meet with his dear friend Levin, who—Cernuda thought—was none other than a thinly veiled version of Leo Tolstoy himself. Barely two minutes into the chapter, and much to his chagrin, Luis encountered this somber passage:

"Well, what of it? I've not given up thinking of death," said Levin. "It's true that it's high time I was dead; and that all this is nonsense. It's the truth I'm telling you. I do value my idea and my work awfully; but in reality only consider this: all this world of ours is nothing but a speck of mildew, which has grown up on a tiny planet. And for us to suppose we can have something great—ideas, work—it's all dust and ashes."

"But all that's as old as the hills, my boy!"

Luis stopped here. To be reading this, right now, on that night? And then, he couldn't stop wondering about his own work, his life's work, *Reality and Desire*—that book of books which he has been working on for many years now, that slice of "unblemished perfection," that "shining star in the firmament of Spanish literature," as Federico once said with exaggerated effusion—was not, ultimately, a blot of mold growing on this tiny planet called Earth, an insignificant grain of sand with no importance whatsoever, as Tolstoy darkly wrote. Yes, that's what it was. As much it hurt him to admit it, *Reality and Desire*, the son of the spirit who carefully watched over him, didn't matter in the least.

He continued reading:

> "It is old; but do you know, when you grasp this fully, then somehow everything becomes of no consequence. When you understand that you will die tomorrow, if not today, and nothing will be left, then everything is so unimportant! And I consider my idea very important, but it turns out really to be as unimportant too, even if it were carried out, as doing for that bear. So one goes on living, amusing oneself with hunting, with work—anything so as not to think of death!"

Again, inevitably, Luis's thoughts were drawn back to Iñaki Sobrino. Tolstoy was right: everything, when you get down to it, is a distraction from death. Everything. Even reading *Anna Karenina* in a country home that isn't mine, even the actual writing of *Anna Karenina*, and the months and years I invested in *Reality and Desire*, however painful it might end up being to either Tolstoy or to me. Reading these few lines about death had, ironically, done it: for a few minutes, he'd forgotten about José, he'd been able to brush away the pending death that hung like a bird of ill omen over little José Sobrino and his poisoned blood.

He continued reading:

"Oh, I don't know. All I know is that we shall soon be dead."

"Why so soon?"

"Don't you know, there's less charm in life, when one thinks of death, but there's more peace."

More peace? Cernuda thought, setting the weighty tome off to one side of the bed, giving up on the reading. Thinking about death can leave me with a greater sense of peace? Could what Levin says with such assurance, such confidence, be true? My God. I have half a mind to ask Iñaki what he thinks about all of that when I go see him tomorrow, but I wouldn't dare. I couldn't. Right now, Luis said to himself, only two things are clear: that I couldn't care less about my own life or death, and that now I feel the full weight of the disease afflicting that young soldier, orphaned by the Battle of Bilbao, hanging over me like a curse.

30

"Do you know who Alessandro Momo is?" asked Jacinto.

Luis and his best friend found themselves sitting on the terrace at the El Péndulo café and bookstore in the Polanco neighborhood of Mexico City. It would have been the summer of 2000 or maybe 2001 but no later than August, since the Twin Towers had yet to be destroyed. El Péndulo served excellent coffee; still, though, you had to know what to order, otherwise they'd bring you what Jacinto referred to with scorn and contempt as "sock water," or weak, tasteless, swill. The proper coffee, preferred by connoisseurs and El Péndulo regulars, was called "illy caffe" and was a special sort of espresso made with boiling water. Every cup is freshly brewed, served hot, and never left to sit in a carafe.

Salerno Insausti had bought a few books that stale morning, including *Sculpting in Time* by Tarkovsky and *Reality and Desire*, which Jacinto said he'd have to read if he didn't want to risk losing his best friend. Luis Cernuda's book contained, for him, some of the best poems ever written in Spanish … verses which he, Jacinto, could only dream of writing. However, truth be told, Luis knew little or nothing about poetry. He appreciated it about as much as he appreciated Baroque music and Fauvism, but there were no forms of art he was more passionate about than photography and cinema. These were his true loves, his whores. Painting, poetry, or music always came in second place, quite different from Jacinto who held poetry above all else, including philosophy and politics. Luis had always been the first and most attentive reader of his childhood friend's poems. Through Jacinto—or through his occasionally delirious poetry—he had acquired a broader, better appreciation of poetry in general. When it came to the Generation of '27 (also known as the Generation of the Republic or the Generation of Friendship), the only one he knew about was the man from Granada, García Lorca, and even then he only knew a dozen or so of his poems. In other words, he knew as much as any other high school student in Mexico who'd spent a week or two in class studying the famous Spanish generation before swiftly moving on to Cela, Matute, and Delibes in one fell swoop. Which is to say, Luis knew next to nothing about the Generation of '27 and that explains why he didn't recognize Luis Cernuda, his namesake, when Jacinto recommended the book, when he pulled *Reality and Desire* off the shelf there at El Péndulo and ordered him to buy it on that distant morning. Many years later, there was one thing he thought he remembered, one particular detail that had caught his attention: that the Sevillian poet had died in exile in Mexico. That was it. And the book he bought on that summer day in 2000 or 2001 would never be opened. It lay, along with many others, on a bookshelf at the home of his parents, or perhaps one of his sisters.

The server brought their two illy caffes up to the terrace where the two young men were lounging in their chairs, radiant and joyful, ready to once again begin the pleasant process of initiating a relaxing conversation. The first thing the server said to Luis was that he need-ed to put out his cigarette … which he did, though with an aggra-vated look on his face, and of course only after taking two last, long puffs. Jacinto chuckled, either at Luis being reprimanded or the an-noyance it caused him, before getting back to the matter at hand:

"So, my film buff friend, do you know who Alessandro Momo is or not?"

"I don't," Luis said as he set his bagged books down on the ground next to his comfortable armchair, with the exception of the Cernuda title, which he placed on a corner of the table. Then he took a sip of his hot, fresh coffee, and asked:

"Okay then, who is this Momo you're talking about? The char-acter from the Michael Ende novel?"

"No, you idiot. That Momo is a children's book character. Ales-sandro Momo was a great Italian actor. You should know these things, Luis. You're the movie expert, not me."

"I had no idea."

"He was my idol," Jacinto affirmed, still without having touched his coffee, brushing his hair off his forehead and adjusting his glasses.

"When I was a teenager."

"So not too long ago," Salerno Insausti scoffed, dispelling his own bad mood with a jab at his friend.

"Shut up and listen ... when I was fourteen, I saw two of Momo's films. In fact, I saw each of them several times over: *Malicious* and *Lovers and Other Relatives*. They were both directed by Salvatore Samperi, a famous director from the seventies."

"I saw *Malicious*."

"No, Luis. You saw *Malice*. The Hollywood *Malice*."

"With Alec Baldwin and Nicole Kidman."

"Yes. But I'm talking about *Malicious*, the one from 1974. The Italian film with Laura Antonelli."

"Yeah, I know who Antonelli is. She's gorgeous."

"I would jerk off to her in those two movies until my dick got sore," Jacinto confessed for no reason other than the excitement of telling Luis. "I was crazy about her. She was like the hot aunt that every teenager wanted to have: beautiful, kind, selfless, loving, tender, feminine, and secretly sensual."

"Okay, great, so what about her?"

"She broke out in 1974, along with Alessandro Momo, a seventeen-year-old kid with the face of a fourteen-year-old. After they made *Malicious* together, they made another film, *Lovers and Other Relatives*, a year later, with the same director."

"And what about your idol, Jacinto?" Luis asked as he tapped his cigarette butt on the ash tray, thinking about lighting it up again and sneaking a few puffs in behind the server's back.

"Momo, or Nino, his character in *Malicious*, is a fourteen-year-old who's in love with Laura Antonelli, just like I was and probably millions of others were as well. I saw him, you know, and imagined that I was the one who was undressing Laura Antonelli, getting her out of her panties, trying to seduce a woman nearly twenty years older. But especially with the first of the two movies — *Malicious* — I've never been able to forget it. I remember everything, down to the last detail, Luis."

"So what's it about?"

"Nino's father, recently widowed, hires a thirty-something nanny to take care of his three motherless children. Alessandro Momo, who plays Nino, is the middle one. The father, a good man with money, depressed over the loss of his wife, begins to fall for Antonelli, as does Nino's older brother, who's about twenty or twenty-one. One way or another, everyone in that house begins to fall for their new nanny's beauty and tenderness. With affection and endearment, she gradually begins to replace their deceased wife and mother. But of all of them, Nino is the most astute, and soon enough he discovers his father's true intentions: marry the nanny and make her their stepmother. Antonelli, for her part, realizes that marrying a rich man with noble intentions like the father isn't such a bad idea. So Nino begins relentlessly asking the nanny for little favors here and there. For example, I remember one scene where he asks her to put on a pair of panties that he saw her ironing one afternoon, and then later he asks her to climb a ladder to get a book down off the top shelf of a bookcase just so he could see whether or not she was actually wearing the panties. She hadn't, of course, and so Nino starts to mess with his five-year-old brother by talking to him, at night, while he's asleep, saying that their mother's spirit still didn't want to leave them, that she didn't want their father to marry this new nanny. The kid starts to have recurring nightmares: he cries all through the night, all because of Nino, though nobody suspects him of anything. A friend of the family—a priest who regularly stops by to see how the four men of the house are handling their loss—learns about these nightmares and recommends that perhaps it's not such a good idea for the father to remarry quite so soon. He hadn't been widowed for even three months yet."

"So through his little brother's nightmares, Nino gets the favors from the nanny ..."

"Antonelli understands the power play that has been set up between her and Nino: if you want to marry my father, you have to agree to my terms. But the funny thing, Luis, is that none of the terms ever involve sex. It's all just a bunch of erotic games and adolescent fantasies in the feverish mind of a teenage virgin."

"In your mind, you mean."

"And in yours too, asshole!" Jacinto interjected, before immediately continuing on, undeterred by the interruption. "The whole movie is based on Nino's ploy."

"And how does it end?"

"Eventually Nino stops secretly tormenting his brother at night, and that allows Antonelli and the father to get married with the priest's blessings. In the end, everyone's happy."

"So that's it?" Luis asks, slightly disappointed, taking his cup of coffee by the handle.

"Of course not," Jacinto said tantalizingly, enjoying the semblance of suspense he'd created. "In the end, after having won over the beautiful nanny, in a juvenile act of power, every erotic demand and occurrence—like, for example, having her remove her panties while at the dinner table with his father, his brothers, and the priest—Antonelli decides that it's now it's time for her to get her revenge on the kid."

"How?"

"She rapes him."

"What?

"Yeah, you heard me right," Jacinto said, grinning, before immediately adding, "Well, it depends on what you mean by rape. In this case, the thirty-year-old woman decides to take Nino's little game to the extreme; in other words, she decides to teach him one hell of a lesson: from the erotic fantasies and flirtations—the source of Nino's power—she goes straight to intercourse in a memorable scene when the house is empty and the lights go out during a torrential thunderstorm."

"Okay, now I'm speechless."

"It's worth seeing, my cinematic scholar. It's really good."

"Oh I'll watch it." After a few moments of reflection and a sip of his coffee, Luis asked, "So why did you want to talk about *Malicious*?"

"Actually I was wondering about whatever happened to this Momo guy. I never saw him in any other films, except for the one I mentioned, *Lovers and Other Relatives*. So I googled him to see what the hell has been going on in his life."

"So what did you find?"

"He died a few days before his twentieth birthday, in November of 1975."

"How?"

"In a damn motorcycle accident."

"So young ..."

"And you know what's worse, Luis? He had just finished filming what would end up being his last and best work: *Scent of a Woman*. Yeah, yeah," he said, anticipating his friend's immediate question. "But this was the original. The Al Pacino film was a remake."

"I had no idea."

"Me either." Jacinto paused for a second before finally adding, "I haven't seen *Scent of a Woman*, but I'm gonna look it up in honor of Alessandro, my childhood hero."

"Let me know when you find it and I'll watch it with you, if you want."

"You know what still gets me though? Momo's death at such a young age. Here I am, one of his many fans, on the other side of the Atlantic, twenty-five years after he died, wondering whatever happened to him, wondering what other movies he might have made with Laura Antonelli ... and what a bitter surprise! Twenty-five years later I learn that my teenage hero died barely a year after filming *Malicious* and *Lovers and Other Relatives*. He never even got to see the final cut of *Scent of a Woman*. Honestly, Luis, I was stunned ... I almost felt like I had been the one who died when I was Nino's age—fourteen—and I'm only finding out about it now on Google. Can you imagine? What a strange feeling."

Luis didn't know how to respond to all of that. He was quite confused. Was he supposed to comfort Jacinto about Alessandro Momo's ancient death? What the hell was he trying to get out of him with this story? He resigned himself to calmly sipping his coffee, a bit frustrated that he couldn't light up another cigarette (now, when he needed it the most) on the terrace there at El Péndulo. He never imagined that just a few years after that stupid ban on smoking in public, places would become so strict: the new global standard leaving no exceptions, for example, in places like the famous café and bookstore there in the Polanco neighborhood of Mexico City. It would also have been impossible to imagine that after this summer morning where, four or five years later, he would be leaving Mexico for a five-year span which, incidentally, would allow him to confirm firsthand that the war on smokers was also raging in the capital of the world, his future home: New York.

"Hey," Jacinto called, drawing him out of his reflections. "Someone's been staring at you for a while now."

"Who?"

"That girl, over to your left," Jacinto said with a quick glance to the side, adjusting his glasses with his ring finger.

Almost involuntarily, Luis turned to his left, and his gaze collided with that of a young, green-eyed girl. He was taken aback; then, suddenly, she smiled at him, and he smiled back. A mimetic, mechanical gesture. The girl, though, never looked away from his profile for even a split second. Luis felt her focusing on him, and couldn't help but look to his left again, over his shoulder: yes, she was still watching him. Did they know one another? No. He was almost certain. Meanwhile, Jacinto couldn't help but smile in amazement, looking back and forth between him and her. The finale, however, came when he saw the girl get up from her seat, leaving her companion behind, red with embarrassment, and start making her way over to their table, cheerful and confident, as if it were no big thing. But did they actually know each other? That's what Jacinto wanted to know. Maybe they did ... his prying gaze was relentless. Then again, maybe they didn't, judging by the look of total bewilderment on Luis's face as he watched her coming, not knowing what the hell to do or even what to say. He and Jacinto were both dumbstruck when she greeted them with a broad, bright smile framed by gently curving red lips:

"Sergio?"

"I'm sorry, but you have me confused with someone else," Luis said, completely unprepared as he stood up from the table.

"I'm sorry … You look just like a friend of mine I haven't seen in years. A boyfriend of mine from school," she corrected herself, blushing. "I really thought it was you," she said, apologizing again before returning to her table without another word.

Sitting stock-still after the encounter, Jacinto and Luis immediately realized that she had lied. Nevertheless, Luis instinctively knew that he had to meet this lovely young woman: he liked her—they liked each other—and she had boldly taken the first step. While Jacinto went to pay the check, Luis got up, went over to her table off in the left hand corner, and asked her if he could call her sometime. If she had been brave enough to pretend to confuse him with someone else, then he could be just as brazen (or foolhardy) to ask for her phone number without hesitation. He had nothing to lose. If she gave it to him, it would mean that he and Jacinto had correctly read the false girlfriend of the false Sergio. And that was it. She gave him her number and Luis—lacking any scrap of paper—wrote it down on the next best thing he had at hand: his brand new copy of *Reality and Desire*. The girl with the incredible, chartreuse-green eyes went by the name of Setefilla. Quite the unusual name. But despite the curiosity it provoked in him, Luis chose not to ask her anything else.

31

"José died, Luis. He's gone, the poor thing …" Salerno felt that ghostly voice coming through his cell phone as if it were a drill boring through his bones, his eardrums. Was it Diana? His mother? Marcela? His cousin Adriana? Amparo? He never found out. He couldn't remember anything else because he didn't hear anything else: his neurotransmitters had been blocked at the cortex of his soul. All he can remember is a female voice giving him the news and everything else was pure sobs … his sobs, the sobs of this other person, this woman, this voice which had called to tell him this, to recount what could never be explained, what could only suffocate, what could cause such a gripping pain that could only be alleviated with one particular weapon, one supremely powerful antidote: time. But time was not on his side, nor was it on the side of Marcela and Augusto, and it was even less so when it came to his beloved (if unknown) nephew who had died much too soon, years too soon, seventy or eighty years, at least … Why so soon?

At that moment, wiping away his tears, with his head turned towards the window, the flight attendant came up to Salerno Insausti and asked him to turn off his cell phone. The flight was about to take off.

32

Finally, Cernuda was able to drift off to sleep and dream despite the frigid air seeping into his room through some crack in the molding or the thin glass of the windowpane. He dreamed about Setefilla, Gilita's nanny, who had told Valeria, the lady of the house, that they were leaving, running away from the wicked Clockmaker, that she must finally admit that she wasn't happy with that bossy, bombastic Old Man. With the money stolen from the secret drawer, the two could fly away, live an easy life, do whatever they wanted to do, meeting men and traveling the world, Paris, Oslo, Havana, Athens, getting drunk on the finest wines, eating to their hearts' content, and not worry about a thing, nothing at all, the least of which was the damn Old Man, her senile husband, as strict as he was, and so stuck in the past, always fixating over the ticking and the tocking, over the exact hours, minutes, and seconds of his clocks, foolishly and blindly obsessing over them despite the fact that they always kept perfect time. Orderly, punctilious, precise ... how could the woman put up with this? Tell me, I don't understand, doña Valeria, how can you bear it? Why don't you free yourself from the horrible yoke? Valeria didn't know how to respond; she was, of course, astonished by the nanny's excessive confidence, but nevertheless, despite it all, Setefilla was right: deep down, she detested that tiresome Old Man, at once malignant, kind-hearted, and sinister. She hated him with every fiber of her being. The Old Man was—how can I explain?—like light and darkness combined, illusions and false hopes, pleasure and pain, reality and desire, ephemeral joys that were always followed by bitterness and strife. That's what the damn Clockmaker was: a farce, an illusion. That's what he had always been to her and to sweet little Gilita. At first, it's true, he appeared to be a good husband, a faithful and honest spouse, but he had profoundly ruined her, so young, still lovely and attractive to many in the town. And now the future of young Gilita, who had only just turned seventeen would soon be destroyed if something wasn't done. She, Valeria, was twenty-eight, and was without a doubt in the prime of life ... There was, of course, Salvador, who wanted her, who would risk his life for just one of her kisses.

Oh, Setefilla, I'm afraid ... what will become of us? Where would we go if we deceive the Master? Madam, madam, with the stolen money we can run away together, far away ... it doesn't matter where. The first thing to do is make the decision to leave him, to abandon the meticulous Old Man who has brought you nothing but ruin, wrinkles, and time, yes, look what you've become, look at yourself in the mirror, you're not the same woman you were yesterday, you're only getting older, just like the Clockmaker. Do you see now? I told you. Look at yourself. Time takes its toll. Your husband may be the best Clockmaker in town, madam, but He neither gives nor forgives time, He does not dispense life and death. These things happen because they simply ... happen. I swear to you. He, with his manias, would of course like to control all the clocks, control each and every hand, every minute and second of your life, of your time, but as cunning as he is, he still cannot care for you, watch over you, love you the way you deserve, old and senile as he is. Don't you see how he's neglected you so much that right under his very nose, he's driven you into the arms of young Salvador? What's that you said, Setefilla? Shut your vulgar mouth; don't be so insolent, we've given you food and shelter, remember? You should have more respect. I'm your boss. So you think I haven't noticed, is that it, madam? You've been sleeping with that young man for some time now, and there's nothing wrong with that: he's quite handsome, the handsomest lad in the village. But now that he's left you, madam, and replaced you with young Gilita, your daughter ... She's not my daughter, Setefilla, you know that. Forgive me, madam, your stepdaughter ... I meant to say your stepdaughter, Ms. Valeria ... And don't remind me again, Setefilla, I'm ordering you, you're killing me, even the simple hint of memory chokes me: I am mortally wounded, destroyed, don't you see? Damn that girl, she stole my lover, she stole my beloved, who was going to say anything, how would anybody know? Tell me, Setefilla, tell me ... I can't tell you more than the two of us already know, just the two things we read in the letter, madam: Gilita bid farewell to you and her father, the Old Clockmaker; now there is nothing left to do, nothing to hold on to, there are no other choices, madam, so come with me, the two of us together can escape this dead town, I'm begging you, we can go from country to country, from city to city, Oslo, Paris, Havana, Athens, drinking wine, knowing men, we have the money from the secret drawer, we don't need any more of the Old Clockmaker's time."

Cernuda opened his bleary eyes wide: he was chilled to the bone. He tried valiantly to recover some fragment of that dream. He couldn't; he cursed his damn pillow. He rubbed his eyes and reached for the lamp. Where the fuck was this iciness coming from? He was completely covered, with two thick blankets on top of him. He nearly leapt out of bed, put on his slippers, went over to the window and confirmed his suspicions: a tiny crack was letting in a slithering thread of frigid wind that had, over the course of the past several hours, turned his bedroom into an ice rink. He tried to block it up, but to no avail. Something was wrong with the sash, or maybe the jambs were warped. The damn Vullionis, he thought as he threw on his overcoat. Now there was no possible chance of going back to sleep. To hell with it. He checked the clock on the nightstand next to his bed: it was twenty past five. Not too bad. He had actually slept for six, almost seven hours. But just at that instant, after setting the clock back down on the nightstand, he remembered his dream and almost laughed out loud at seeing the image of the Old Clockmaker reflected in the windowpanes. Ah, my Clockmaker, he said, where is my damn Clockmaker? Where did I leave you? He turned to the side, approached his narrow bed, and checked the larger of his two suitcases (his only two possessions in his life), only to find a few clean clothes mixed in with a pile of dirty ones. Then he turned to the smaller of his two bags, unlatched one of the side closures, and there—hidden among the handwritten sheets of paper, strands of tobacco, and a notebook—he found the neatly typed pages of the only piece of work he had ever dared to write for the stage ... driven, perhaps, by the example set by the murder of his best friend:

The Clockmaker or the Family Interrupted: A Fantasy of Providence. After settling back into bed, still shivering, he prepared himself to reread, with pen in hand, the first few pages of this comedy that he had only just finished back in October or November, and had only read at the Congress of Anti-Fascist Writers, and later in Barcelona, just days before crossing the border with his friend Bernabé.

Even so, he thought to himself, smiling as he mended an adjective, this little play isn't too bad; of course, this damn Clockmaker needs a good, strong hand, but, all in all, it's better than I thought. Setefilla, especially, turned out fairly well.

33

As soon as he arrived at the Mexico City airport, Luis dialed his sister Diana's cell phone. Surprised to hear that Luis had come back and was actually there, she explained that they had all left the hospital and were now gathered at Augusto and Marcela's house holding wake over José before he was to be cremated the next day at noon. Neither of them spoke so much as another word. Luis didn't ask, and they left it hanging: the word "cremate" was burning in his ears, and it continued to ring in his head for a long time after. Salerno Insausti made his way to the kiosk where the cab tickets were sold. He checked the time on his watch: it was 2:10 in the morning, and there was next to nobody there at the gate or anywhere at the concourse. Fortunately, there wasn't much of a line at the taxi stand, and in just a couple of minutes, Luis was in a cab. He gave the name of the street to the driver and immediately lost himself in thought, staring out the open window at the dull, lifeless sky, the buildings, the food stands thronged with people, as a biting wind (though not as cold as it was in Manhattan) smacked him in the face and ruffled his hair. Five years. Five years had passed ... He could still feel the salt from the tears he'd shed upon his cheekbones, but there was no crying now, he just needed a breath of air, just enough to keep on living, to keep from choking on the pain.

He heard the driver's voice barking at him as he was still trying to hold onto a sliver of the dream he had succumbed to during his trip: waking up in the hotel room to find that she (and who was she?) wasn't there, she was gone, and that bothered him, it bothered the guy in the dream. Where had she gone? How could she have left him there, alone? In his dream, Luis dressed slowly despite a crushing headache; then he washed his face in the pink granite sink, calmly dried himself off, and walked out of that strange hotel without ever looking back, never to see her again ... The driver barked at him a second time, but who was she, he continued to wonder, stubbornly, almost desperately, without opening his eyes, without even bothering to acknowledge the cabbie ... But there was no hope of finding out now: he was completely awake. Looking out the window, he confirmed that they had arrived; he must have been quite exhausted, because it hadn't even felt like thirty minutes in the cab. The dream must have lasted at least that long. He got out, placed his small suitcase on the ground, and gave the young man a five dollar bill. And with that, the driver vanished into the night. Salerno rubbed his eyes and looked at the sky: the moon — the same full moon that shone over Manhattan — was looking back at him, or at least that's how he felt for a few fleeting seconds while the sound of a motorcycle passed in the distance. As soon as he rang the doorbell, Luis realized what he already knew yet had kept buried until then: that he had never even met and yet still loved, from the distance of his exile in New York, Marcela's youngest son. Remembering that black hole (that empty memory) startled him, frightened him even. He heard his sister's voice over the intercom. It's me, Luis stammered, and a few seconds later Augusto appeared to unlock the front gate. Upon seeing him, upon seeing each other, and without saying so much as a word, his brother-in-law let out a piercing yowl not unlike the howling of a wolf. They hugged. How much time passed as they stood there, locked in that embrace? Augusto wouldn't let go, clinging to Luis with both arms as if he were his only hope, weeping and wailing the name of his child, José, his little José ...

After crossing the front patio and entering the home, Luis could just barely make out, there, in the darkened living room, a small box with an open lid surrounded by candles; he could discern people he recognized and people he didn't standing with their backs to the walls; he could distinguish some washed-out, ashen faces, a number of standing figures and others sitting down, crushed, lost, spectral, heads and necks buckling, and all of them either silent or sobbing ... That was the scene he took in there in the burning darkness, a scene he would never forget for the rest of his life.

As he was about to approach the casket, blindly groping his way as if to avoid falling into the abyss, Luis felt two burning arms embrace him out of the thin air, the body of a woman whose smell he'd known since childhood, a bright face streaked with tears dampening his own tear-stained cheeks, and the voice of Marcela, his little sister, pleading, bewailing: "My José, my little José, he's gone ... Luis, José's dead, did you hear me? He left us ... Tell me, Luis, why? Why? Tell me, I'm begging you ... My God, why? José, my little one, my angel, he's gone ..." Behind Marcela's back, behind her flushed face, and without even realizing it, he saw the blurred image of his father and mother embracing in the other corner of the room. Despite the penumbra, their eyes eventually collided. Five years had passed since they'd last spoken. Five years since that last conversation, since that fight or whatever it was that blew up between them and drove them apart for half a decade. He couldn't look at his; he shut his eyes tightly and continued to embrace Marcela, to soak in her pain, her sword, her anger, there beside the candles and the little open casket, so close to the tiny body of José, Marcela's youngest son, his (inexplicably) dead nephew.

Unlike the others gathered there in that congested room, Luis's anger was directed inwardly, only at himself. He had never even met José. Not once. And the profundity of that thought weighed on him more with each passing second; it welled up in his body like a toxic pus. He had chosen to spend those five years in Manhattan, stewing in his foolish anger, the resentment he harbored towards his father and Diana. He had chosen to curse their conspiracy of silence for half a decade instead of returning to Mexico sooner and getting to know his nephew, Fernando's younger brother. And now José was dead, gone from the land of the living, nonexistent. Now he would never see him again. Or would he? But how, if he never saw him before, if they never even met, he thought with a fright, how could he see him *again*? What the fuck are you thinking, Luis?

Now, if there were anything left to do, it was to see whether Father Time would allow him to live and breathe peacefully.

With a tremendous, superhuman effort, Salerno approached the little wooden casket. He saw him there, beautiful, peaceful, without breathing or begging anyone for even one more drop of sand in the hourglass ... and Luis saw himself, the same pallid face that he'd had at that age.

34

One Easter weekend Luis and Jacinto took off for Acapulco. It was, in fact, a last minute decision. Jacinto suggested the idea after a friend of his mother's (perhaps even the same friend from the sauna at the country club, the same woman through whom he first learned about Luis's half sister) left him the keys to her condo in Caleta. They were both well aware of the fact that Caleta didn't have anything close to the best beaches and that there were more popular nightclubs elsewhere in Acapulco, but that didn't matter ... it was a splendid, even luxurious place, and it had a pool that overlooked a spectacular view. At night, after spending the day at the always fashionable Hotel Elcano, lying out under the sun, reading, and letting their minds wander, they went back to the condo to clean up and get all decked out before heading to the Palladium, the impressive club located atop the Las Brisas hillside, overlooking the Miguel Alemán promenade. From there, through the massive, twenty-foot-tall glass windows, they would contemplate, while couples danced the night away, arm in arm, the infinite line of dazzling hotels lining the coast as far as Caletilla and beyond even that.

They had been drinking vampiros and clamato juice since noon, which is when they arrived at the Elcano ready to relax and sunbathe; later, at sunset, they switched to beers on the deck of the pool back at the complex, and finally, with dinner, they dispatched a couple bottles of perfectly chilled red wine along with their pasta with arrabiata sauce, which Jacinto had prepared with shrimp, tomatoes, and basil. Later that same Friday night, once they had reached the top of the Las Brisas hillside and overcome the biggest obstacle of all (actually gaining entrance to the Palladium), Jacinto and Luis continued in synchronized adherence to their tireless, ethylic march involving tequilas, beers, and cuba libres: an ominous yet effective combination of alcohol. By about two in the morning, the two friends had consubstantiated with the crowd that had gathered there in the name of music and dance: all were brothers,

and the universe itself was in the same state of delightful Diony-
sian drunkenness. Jacinto and Luis had each danced with a number
of girls since the dance floor was opened at eleven; some of them
they'd asked to dance, while others they'd simply met out there on
the floor, dancing body to body, skin to skin, without much to say
or even much desire to talk but, yes, indeed, with the desire to lose
themselves in each other, to become one, to abandon the body and
the consciousness for just one night. The Palladium was packed:
servers came and went through narrow aisles carrying trays of bottles and glasses, groups of sweet smelling girls moved from one table
to another, from one corner of the room to another, from one bar
to another, looking for some hot young man or some lost friend
caught up in the bacchanal, or perhaps just to exhibit their turgid
forms in hopes of attracting a Don Juan or a Prince Charming. The
men, meanwhile, were checking out the young ladies, examining
them in the dark to determine whether they wanted to ask them to
dance, while other men and women went alone to the dance floor
by themselves, confident in their chances of finding another body
there, any body with bronzed skin to touch and grind against, and
maybe even a set of lips to kiss later that night.

Between drinks, Jacinto said to Luis:

"Remember what they say: all chicks look the same when the
lights go out. So be careful, mi amigo."

They both laughed.

And it was true. No matter how hard they squinted, they couldn't
make out anything more than blurred faces and faded, phantasma-
goric bodies, all mixed up in the commotion of dancing and thundering music, colorful glowsticks, and a strident, pounding bass line
that made the walls and high ceiling of the club shake.

"I'm gonna go dance," Luis shouted in Jacinto's ear, trying to
break through the wall of sound.

"What?" he replied, still not having understood Luis despite his
best efforts.

"I'm gonna go dance," he shouted, even more loudly.

"With who?"

"Nobody," Luis replied, leaving his empty glass in his friend's hand.

Alone, working his way through the crowd, forging a path through the indistinguishable mass of humanity, Luis eventually reached the dance floor and decided to trip the light fantastic all by himself to that old Phil Collins song he liked so much. He was drunk. He knew it. But not completely ... because he was aware—despite everything, including his body—of how he felt, of how everything was reeling around him, and how his head was spinning along with the human whirlwind. If I didn't realize what was going on around me, then I would be completely drunk; that was his obvious conclusion, the logic that could never deceive him. So he let himself be carried off by the music, closing his eyes for a while, happy simply to exist or joyous in feeling that that night didn't exist for anyone, that his body wasn't his body anymore but an emptiness, that he was alive outside of his flesh and his skeleton, that perhaps he was living in all the other bodies around him just as the others were living in him without even imagining it. Nobody was a stranger there: he was everyone. He was no one. Luis was not Luis.

Suddenly, his eyes still closed, he felt a hand on his shoulder, gently squeezing it. He looked: he knew her, he'd seen her before. Of course I recognize that face, he said to himself in a flash, but who is she? Where the hell do I know her from? He had an image of her inside of himself, right on the tip of his tongue, ready to sprout forth, but he couldn't assemble the parts nor reconstruct her gentle features, he was stuck in his drunkenness until a flash of light from the disco ball illuminated the chartreuse-green eyes of the young woman and immediately he remembered that look, those lips, those eyebrows, but not a name or a place.

"Do you remember me?"

"Of course," Luis lied, for although he recognized those green eyes, he didn't know where or when he'd seen them before, nor did he remember the name of this apparition.

"How are you?" she shouted, still dancing with Luis to the Phil Collins song.

"I'm good ..."

"I can see ..."

"What?" Luis shouted, not having heard her.

"You look really happy."

"Yeah," Luis replied, a bit dazed and suddenly less drunk. "How are you?"

"Great."

"Who are you here with?" He wanted to use her name, but Luis still couldn't remember it. Still, though, she was being friendly and casual with him, so he was doing the same with her.

"Just some girlfriends. We came down for the weekend. You know, to party."

"Us too," Luis shouted, trying to be heard over the music and the noise of the crowd.

"You're here with friends?" she asked, leaning closer towards Luis's ear, almost grazing his earlobe with her lips. "The one you were with at El Péndulo?"

And that, finally was the key: those glaucous eyes, those thin lips, that unvarnished skin, that smile, those eyebrows ... he knew them from the bookstore in Polanco. Of course.

"Yeah," Luis replied. "With Jacinto."

Without another word, the two of them continued dancing, surrounded by the hundreds of others dancing around them, everyone bumping and grinding, mixing together in a mortar of flesh and sweat. Then, after a few minutes of keeping time with the music—magnetized by this mutual understanding—she said to him in a voice just loud enough to be heard:

"You never called me."

Taken aback, not remembering the real reason, Luis responded with the first thing that popped into his head, almost embarrassed:

"I'm sorry, I couldn't find your number." Was that a lie? Was it true? Luis had no idea. He didn't even remember whether he actually looked for it and couldn't find it, or if he simply forgot about this girl the same day he met her at El Péndulo.

"It doesn't matter," she laughed, pressing her body against his while still moving, still dancing. "That was a couple years ago, right?"

"Yeah," Luis said, not sure of how much time had passed since then, how much had actually transpired, all the while leaning his freshly shaven face closer to the young woman, looking at her steadily despite the darkness and the noise, almost certain that he could kiss her, just waiting for the perfect moment, knowing instinctively that's what she wanted, that's why she had been dancing with him for the past fifteen or twenty minutes, pressing her body into his, her hips gyrating against him in a sort of rising feminine tide, swinging and swaying in time with the rest of the crowd there on the dance floor. It was just a matter of deciding when ... Luis was on the verge of kissing her, yes, now, he was just waiting for the human wave to roll back and he would do it.

"I bet you don't even remember my name." Luis wasn't expecting this, just as he was about to grab her around the to waist make his move.

"Huh?" he asked, confused, leaning nearer to her ear as if he hadn't quite heard her, being carried away by the high-decibel music blaring over the dance floor.

"Nothing," she said, and continued to dance, looking towards the windows now, then to the crowd, and finally back to Luis, taking him in with her green eyes, studying him as if she might have loved him once, or as if she might want to love him again, on some dim and distant day in the future.

But why him, why Luis? Why do I like this girl? he asked himself with suspicion. In his heart, Luis knew that she had chosen him a long time ago, ever since that meeting at the café in Polanco, though he didn't know why, he didn't understand, and that was what scared him. Just a slight twinge, but it vanished as soon as she grabbed his arms and stretched her body up straight, bringing her chin up to the level of his. Luis, defenseless, feeling the last fiber of ephemeral fear rushing out of his body, kissed her. It was a long kiss, a kiss in motion, even though they both (instinctively) had managed to slow down their rhythms to avoid any complications, to keep from dislocating their lips, and perhaps to discover the taste of each other's tongue and saliva.

"You know, I love your eyes," Setefilla said once the osculation was over, though without letting go of him, her arms still wrapped around his neck. "Ever since I first saw you, I've loved your eyes."

"You're so beautiful," replied Luis.

The rest was fleetingly quick and hard to delineate, even if he tried. Things happened, fragments and sensations, but amidst the mutual fondling, the kisses and the music, among the hundreds of delicate bodies dancing in the darkness, below the neon lights and the glittering disco balls, it was impossible for Luis to discern any order, any sort of syntax: everything had been superimposed, every episode, every event from that night seemed to be one single unity, an immense avalanche, or better yet, a massive wave of fire, unstoppable and impossible to explain. If he were to link those moments together, each sequence as it happened, we would have to say that the two of them continued to dance together for about an hour during which time Luis forgot about Jacinto and Setefilla forgot about her friends, that they had drink after drink in different corners of the club, that they continued kissing and groping one another, that they finally left together, arm in arm, drunk and furtive, without telling anyone, escaping the crowd, that they caught a cab, that they went back to the girl's hotel room, the girl with the green eyes, the chartreuse eyes, like the liquor they drank at the bar, toasting their health, when Luis kissed her on the eyelids, that they slept together, that they fucked, enraptured, drunk with desire despite the exhaustion, until they finally drifted off into a deep sleep, their bodies still intertwined.

35

That Thursday, Cernuda walked down the lane flocked with cuckoo birds, just as he did every morning. He'd promised Iñaki that he'd read him a few of his poems, which is why he had, under his arm, a well-worn first edition copy of *Reality and Desire*, the same first edition copy that his friend Bergamín had given him hot off the press, back in April of 1936. At the last moment, standing at the door about to his house, he thought about bringing a draft of "The Fountain," that little poem which had been inspired by a walk in the Luxembourg Garden back in mid-March, shortly before leaving France and coming to England. Other than a longer poem dedicated to Aleixandre, it was the last thing he had written. But in the end he decided against it. "The Fountain" and the other texts (which were still just rough drafts) were not, perhaps, the best reading for that particular occasion which looked to be a difficult one, considering it involved a child with leukemia. "Lament and Hope," "To Larra, With Violets," "Dreaming of Death"—all of these would perhaps, someday in the not too distant future, form a new chapter in *Reality and Desire*, the most mournful and miserable pages he had ever written in his life. Which is why he thought it would be best to read some of his older work to José, something from his early years, when he was more juvenile and still had hopes for and even believed in mankind and love.

He spent the morning in the usual commotion, getting the youngest children ready for class and getting ready for the day: he helped them into their raggedy outfits, then he wrapped up the bundles of dirty clothes which the assistants would send off to be cleaned at a commercial laundry service. Then, after washing the littlest ones' bleary faces, he helped to serve the meager breakfast in the spacious dining hall: a glass of milk to each child along with a crust of bread and occasionally a piece of chocolate or a hard-boiled egg. It wasn't much, but it seemed to keep them satisfied until noon, when they received another ration of bread and boiled potatoes or beans. The children spent their mornings in different classrooms, and Luis was instructing the older ones in his, teaching them what he wanted and what he could. If it wasn't too cold—if the sun ever decided to come out that month of May—they would take them out into the countryside to play games and make up stories there under the white poplar trees.

But all morning, he couldn't help but think of Iñaki: almost against his will, he had promised to go visit him at the hospital in Oxford that afternoon. Despite his genuine desire to see the boy again, Cernuda still felt a small, indescribable sense of suffering at the knowledge of the state he would find him in: gaunt, weak, in helpless agony. It wasn't just the recently-acquired obligation that spurred him to go, but also (and on the contrary, it seemed) it was his intense desire to see those green eyes that seemed to bore right into him, reading him, knowing him: a look that seemed to know something about his (shared) tragic destiny.

Finally, and after asking the house porter to call a car for him, Cernuda was taken to the hospital. He could have walked to the train station, and walked the rest of the way from there, if it hadn't been for the fatigue that was beginning to set in as he left the farm-house with the copy of his book under his arm. It was four in the afternoon. As the car pulled up, he felt a knot beginning forming in his throat, a thick knot that could not be undone. For a second, he thought about asking the driver to take him back to the farmhouse or to the Vullioni's home, but he dismissed the thought when faced with the searing memory of Iñaki asking him to bring a few poems, to read something to him that afternoon.

When he got to the hospital, walking down one of the corridors leading to José Sobrino's room, he saw a child about ten years of age, and this time he recognized him. It was Luis, José's younger brother. He had met him some time ago, and Iñaki had mentioned him the previous day: Luis Sobrino had written a poem to his mother, and had read it for Cernuda soon after he arrived. Of course. Also, he had his older brother's eyes: green, though they were of a darker shade. They saw one another. Luis, the younger one, seemed to recognize him and approached him calmly and quietly. Cernuda extended his hand:

"How are you?" he said in greeting. "You're Luis, Iñaki's brother, right?"

"Yes."

"Do you remember me?"

"Of course," he replied, his voice a bit sad, subdued.

"Have you seen your brother?"

"Yes, just a little bit ago. He's waiting for you. He wasn't sure whether you were going to keep your promise."

"Of course I am. I haven't forgotten."

"You know, he's going to be really happy to see you. He said he felt a little lonely all day, even though I was with him the whole time. We always talk about our parents, about the kilns where they work, about school in Bilbao, about our friends ... then we think back over birthdays and parties, saddling up the colts and riding them, playing around over by the old tower, and the thousands of other things that happened before we ended up here ..."

"It's good of you to be with him," was all Cernuda could manage to say.

"You look really tired," the boy said, and after a few long moments of absolute silence with the two Luises standing there face to face in the sleek, Lysol-scented hallway, little Luis Sobrino said to Luis Cernuda: "You know something? Iñaki said goodbye to me today. I don't know why. He was acting all strange, stranger than normal ... I told him that tomorrow I'd come and see him again just like I always do, that he should stop talking like that, that everything was going to be okay, that Mom would be furious if she heard him talking like that ..."

Luis didn't have words. Instead of crying, he embraced his little namesake, who barely reached his waist. He hadn't hugged anybody in quite some time. Not even Stan.

"Go on now. Don't worry. Your brother is going to be fine."

Luis Sobrino didn't respond. He just kept on walking down the hallway to where the young nurse from Almería, whom Cernuda had also met not long ago, was waiting for him.

Just before he was about to enter Iñaki's room, he saw, just a few steps away, one of the priests who had arrived from Spain with the children and who, like him, had been working with the members of the Basque Children's Committee. The young man of the cloth, with whom Cernuda had never exchanged so much as a single word, was softly complaining to one of the nurses, who also spoke Spanish:

"He's refused for the third time now. He won't let me give him his last rites, and he doesn't want to confess. This little boy is being very stubborn. So you know what I did? I showed him this . . ." Here he lifted the large black crucifix that was dangling from his gray cassocks. "I said, 'Take a good look, my son, I'm begging you.' And do you know what he said? You won't believe this . . . 'Oh my God, that's ugly.' Yes, he really said that. Dear Lord, if that's not the worst of it . . . What kind of religion did this poor soul receive in Bilbao?"

Cernuda, who was silently listening in on this conversation with his back to them, was about to turn around and interject: Nothing. Thank God, no religion was given. It's because of that religion you practice, and because of all the other religions that don't commune with yours, that José's father is dead and that Spain is dead and that were are all scattered across this world, starving, on the verge of death . . . don't you see? But then he thought, while still not daring to voice it: José isn't being stubborn or obstinate. It's called integrity, and the two of you just don't understand it.

Sick of listening to them, he entered Iñaki's room.

The child's eyes lit up upon seeing him: once again, he found himself face to face with those green irises that bore ever so deeply into him. When he saw this glaucous glow, Luis realized just how glad he was to see José again, to confirm that he was there, alive. The nurse entered the room behind him without uttering a word. Despite the fatigue that patently showed in Iñaki's body (his purplish lips, his face more pale and spent than the previous day), the boy smiled when he saw him standing in the doorway.

"Come in," he murmured. "Sit down."

"How are you feeling, Iñaki?" Luis asked as he drew a wrought iron chair up alongside the bed.

"I didn't think you were coming."

"Well I'm here now, and I've brought what you asked for ..." He showed the boy his tattered copy of *Reality and Desire*, wondering whether he should lean over and actually hand it to him, but Cernuda decided against it; Iñaki hadn't reached for it, being scarcely able to crack a smile of gratitude. Then Luis said, "I saw your brother ..."

"Yes, he was here."

Luis thought about gently cautioning or reproaching him, asking him why he had said goodbye to Luis in such a way, that it wasn't right, that his little brother was a bit sad when he left, that he, Iñaki, would get better, that it was just a matter of time, of being patient ... He wanted to say all of this, but Cernuda chose to keep his mouth shut. What good would any of his words do? What good was his life? Choking back his own anger was the only answer to his question.

Finally, after a short time during which Iñaki closed his eyes and lay there motionless, Cernuda made a sound: just an articulation of his neck or a shrug of his shoulders, a momentary little creak or pop, and that was enough for José to open his eyes again.

"Please don't go," the boy begged. "I'm just tired, but please, read to me, read something, please."

"Of course," Cernuda replied, opening his book, searching for an appropriate poem, growing upset that he couldn't find anything to read to the boy, until finally, after flipping through page after page, he found one. Yes, he would read this one, titled "We Never Plan on Love." He began:

That night the sea couldn't sleep.
Tired of counting, endlessly counting the waves
It wanted to live somewhere far away
Where it could learn something of its own bitter color.

With an insomniac tongue, it muttered vague phrases.
Ocean liners softly crossed paths

In the depths of night,
Their pale bodies, dressed in the clothes of oblivion,
Voyaging towards nothingness.

The sea sang storms, it thundered torrents
Beneath darkening skies,
Like darkness itself,
Like eternal darkness,
Ever resentful of birds and stars.

Its voice journeyed on across lights, across rain and cold,
To reach those cities raised up in the clouds:
Serene Sky, Colored Canyon, Glaciers of Hell,
All made of pure snow, of stars fallen
Into earth's frail hands.

But the sea grew weary of waiting for the cities.
Over there, its loneliest love was but a vague pretext,
An outdated smile,
Unseen by all.

And, dreaming anew, it slowly returned
To where nobody
Knows anything of anyone.
Where the world comes to an end.

When he was done reading, Luis looked up at José, perhaps to see whether an impression had been left on the young boy's face, and to his relief there was one: a smile. It was the tiniest grimace of joy, of fatigue and of thanks to the damned poet for bothering to take the time out of his life to come visit him at the hospital, to read something to him.

Suddenly, drawing him out of his drowsiness or his ponderings, he heard the weak yet clear voice of Iñaki Sobrino.

"Now, please, don't go just yet, but I'm going to turn towards the wall here so that you don't see me die."

Both Cernuda and the nurse, who was still standing there silently behind him, thought this was a joke. Neither of them moved so much as a finger: their hearts froze as they held their breath. They waited, motionless.

A few seconds later, they heard a long, guttural snort.

The child had died.

36

The crematorium on Calzada de Tlalpan was in an old house from the Porfirio regime with bougainvilleas and honeysuckles climbing up the whitewashed walls, surrounded by trees, while the rest of the property was covered in gardens of mid-sized and well-pruned shrubs planted in symmetrical patterns. To the left, and directly across from the sprawling house, you could see the cars and trucks, the ambulances and minibuses, speeding down the broad avenue: hundreds of transitory commuters passing through the milky gray smog and the infernal noise of the city. Still, though, the funeral home and crematorium made at least some effort to shelter them from the congestion and the worldly racket there in that lush little sanctuary located right in the heart of the urban jungle. For some reason, city dwellers seem to forget that they, too, will one day die. No small wonder, then, that the place was called Eternal Rest.

When Luis arrived there with Cirilo, he didn't know what to make of the name. The place, though, seemed pleasant enough: it was immaculate, a fine, quiet place to mark a painful and unprecedented passing, or worse: a place to perform a strange human custom of unknown origins. He didn't know whether it was better, not as bad, or just as appropriate as the alternative. Cremation—a descendent of those ancient funeral pyres—and turning the dead into dust, creating a pile of ashes, reducing matter into another form, something lighter, more simple that cannot decay ... was that what they meant by "eternal rest," Luis asked himself.

A woman led him and Cirilo to a room decorated with earthenware vases and urns filled with white lilies and gardenias, where Augusto and Paco, his best friend, were already waiting. That was all. The four men. They shook hands and embraced without so much as a word before returning to their seats. It was only just a few hours ago that they had been together in the darkness of Augusto's house, and now they were together again at the crematorium in the morning light. Augusto's friend sat next to him on the sofa, with his arm around his shoulder. Luis saw Paco's fingers gently massaging his brother-in-law's back. He felt a tightness in his chest. Cirilo looked at Luis: he wasn't questioning him, but simply commiserating with Augusto's suffering through this look of mutual understanding.

Suddenly, three of the four heard a scream tear through the silence of the room: "My José, my Josesito, where have you gone? Why did you leave us? My God, José ... You can't go ..."

Augusto was staring at the floor while at the same time pounding himself in the temples with clenched fists. Everyone was trying to hold back tears. Luis also balled up his fists as tightly as he could, unable to lift his eyes from the ground. His head was spinning and he hadn't slept at all the night before, even after he left Marcela's house. His eyelids were drooping heavily, though not from exhaustion but rather from so much crying at the side of the little casket. He felt as if his eyes were bloodshot after all the tears but he had no way to know. If he found himself in front of a mirror, he'd check. He'd left his apartment in New York twelve hours ago, and twelve hours later here he was.

A man in a suit and tie entered the room and asked the father of the deceased to come and identify the child before the cremation could begin. It wasn't necessary, but it was a legal issue. One last bitter pill to swallow, which perhaps was why there was nobody besides the four of them there at the time. Augusto stood up on wobbly legs; his friend took him by the arm.

"Would you come with me?" Augusto asked between sobs.

"Of course."

Cirilo and Luis got up, walked over to Augusto and Paco, and they all followed the man through a series of twisting corridors that led to the covered patio that had been converted into a crematorium. That must be what it was, Luis thought. He hadn't known what to expect; he'd never even pictured a crematorium before, let alone set foot in one. It was quite simple: an enormous steel oven firmly set up against one of the walls. That was it. Nothing more. To one side of the oven, José's casket rested on a litter. The man opened the lid; Augusto approached it, looked inside for a moment or two, and bent down to kiss his son. Then Luis did the same, followed by Paco and finally Cirilo. The man closed the casket, opened the oven door, and asked Paco and Cirilo if they would help Augusto back to the waiting room. Luis got up to go with them, but the man asked him to please stay. Once the three men had left the patio, Luis watched the man in the suit and his assistant ease the little casket containing the body of his nephew into the oven. Then they closed the door. The assistant pressed a button and the echo of the flames — the roaring of the flames — grew louder, resounding through the air in hot, concentric waves.

Luis, meanwhile, could still feel that final kiss on his lips. The taste of it, the smell of that last touch. It was hot. Was it the time of day, or was it the oven? Unable to restrain his tears any longer, Salerno Insausti staggered out of there on unsteady feet, winding his way through the empty white hallways. When he got back to the waiting room, Cirilo, Augusto, and his friend were there, sitting in the same spots as before. It was strange: even there they could hear the muffled roar of the oven despite the thick walls and lengthy hallways separating them from the patio. Now it was simply a matter of waiting for the father to receive the urn filled with his son's ashes so they could leave.

It was then that Luis inexplicably remembered the words of a young scientist who'd appeared on the Discovery Channel to explain how every time we drink a glass of water we are actually drinking the atoms of dinosaurs, atoms that made up the bodies of creatures that haven't walked upon this earth for millions of years; then he added that everything in this universe is in a constant state of being recycled, that nothing ever perishes, that the molecules that comprise matter are simply transformed, the same old refrain that his elementary school teacher had repeated ad infinitum and which he had never fully understood until today ... until today? Can just thinking you understand be a form of consolation? Does it remedy anything to know that there is no "eternal rest," that it is simply "eternal recycling," that we never perish and instead are simply converted into something else? That our matter is first diluted throughout the universal sea before being reformed into a new, different, previously nonexistent form of matter, a new form of energy, perhaps on another world, in a different galaxy, thousands of millions of years after this little planet has disappeared from the cosmos entirely? But what about our consciousness, he suddenly wondered. Where will my consciousness be? Where will it go? Will all of these thoughts be reduced to ashes and dust, along with my cerebellum, my hypothalamus, my frontal lobe?

An hour later, the same man in the coat and tie reappeared in the waiting room holding a small, silver urn. Everyone stood up. Augusto meekly received what remained of his son José: the ashes, the dust, the matter, the molecules, the atoms of energy . . .

And now it was time to pay the bill before exiting out the front door.

37

He couldn't stand England. He couldn't stand the children. He couldn't stand his work. He couldn't stand life. He couldn't even put up with himself. Luis Cernuda never went back to that farmhouse, he never said goodbye to any of the assistants, nurses, or the directors of the Basque Children's Committee with whom he'd been working for the previous five or six weeks. He had neither the strength nor the will to do it. Nor did he have the courage to look for his namesake, Luis Sobrino, though he was on the verge of doing so the following morning, after he had said goodbye to the Vullionis, his bags packed, ready to escape his tragedy, believing that there, with José's death, his troubles would be over.

He had barely slept; he'd spent his final night in Oxfordshire brooding in his bed, staring at the wall, recreating those last few moments with Iñaki in his memory, reliving every expression, each and every one of his words out of the few they exchanged, and especially the end. He still couldn't believe what he'd seen there, right before his very own eyes, just a few feet away from him, and yet still completely helpless to do anything, anything at all to stop the cold clutches of death. He was at once terrified and furious, though he sensed that—more than fright—he had had been seized by a completely different feeling. This time, it was much worse than the fear of facing death or life: those two companions that followed him wherever he went like a couple of lapdogs. Now, the thing that overwhelmed him, that cast a pall over him, was his complete and total indifference towards both. And if there were anything to add to that indescribable feeling, it would be bitterness. He might have felt it for years, but now it had been distilled, purified, scarring him for life. He despised having to be a part of this world. He detested it. Perhaps the one thing he didn't hate with all his heart and soul was the ephemeral comfort of seeking out fleeting beauty and settling down to write: two trivial exercises which nevertheless gave him some relief when he had the time to pick up a pen and lose himself in a sheet of paper. It enabled him to forget about this despicable world. But no. That wasn't what he forgot about. He forgot about himself, he ceased to exist, and his pain gave way, it was held up or spread out in the ink.

That's what he did. He took a few smooth, clean pages from his desk drawer and pulled a pen from his jacket pocket. And that night—on into the next morning—he wrote a beautiful poem. He titled it "Ode on the Death of a Basque Boy in England." He re-wrote it three times over, and finally, exhausted, stowed the final version away along with the rest of his personal items. Before bidding the English couple farewell, he was able to catch four hours of sleep.

38

Luis got in the car with Cirilo, who asked him where he was going, where he should drop him off. Salerno didn't know what to say. He was still too shocked and saddened. The experience at the crematorium that morning had left him listless, and yet still he hadn't caught a wink of sleep. Just an overwhelming, pervasive sense of exhaustion. Cirilo asked him again, this time while offering a cigarette. He truly didn't know how to respond. Where should he go, what was he supposed to do now that he had no more business to attend to in Mexico, now that his mission, the reason for his return, had been completed? His nephew was dead and he was nearing his fortieth birthday without any idea whatsoever of what to do with his life.

"Should I take you to Marcela's house, Luis?"

"Yes, thanks," he replied robotically.

He doesn't remember what, if anything, he said to his former brother-in-law, what they might have spoken about during the drive. Perhaps he simply smoked for the entire forty minutes, until Cirilo stopped the car, gave him a hug, and said goodbye.

"I'm heading to work. I'll see you before you go."

"Of course," Luis said, getting out of the car at the exact same place where the cab driver had dropped him off just a few hours before. And he couldn't help but wonder what the hell Cirilo had meant when he said "before you go." Yes, what did that mean, he thought, this whole "I'm going" thing? Where do I have to be right now? While buzzing the intercom for the second time on that short day, he thought, Should I go to New York? Is that it? Go back to New York? I guess that's where I'm headed: a place where nobody's waiting for me, just my Turkish coffee, my computer, my camera, my clothes, my books, and my sublet apartment. All the things I do not love. Of course, he thought. That's the only thing that Cirilo could have been talking about when he said, "before you go." That's what he meant. Nothing more.

The old housekeeper was the only one home. She let him in. Luis went into the backyard, looking at the toys lying there in the grass: a plastic slide, a deflated ball, a few toy swords, two tricycles, a plastic table and set of chairs ... in other words, José's belongings, his legacy. The tears started to flow. He didn't want to see any more. He went back in the house. It was the same as yesterday — the same as it had been a few hours ago — just without the people, the clamor, the sputtering candles, and the coffin. After the housekeeper disappeared back into the laundry room, he went upstairs. He went into the first room he found and laid down on the bed. Off to one side, he saw his carry-on bag waiting for him. His sister must have left it here. He remembered he hadn't brushed his teeth since he left Manhattan. He'd have to do that. He would also have to have a hot shower and try to nap for a bit. Then he would call his mother, Amparo, and Jacinto. His friend, of course, wouldn't know anything; he had neither any reason to wonder nor any way to find out what was going on. He had to see him, he had to talk to him, he had to cry with him.

Opposite the unmade bed, Luis noticed a bookcase built into the wall with a television set in the middle of it. Still holding his toothbrush, undecided as to whether to shower now or rest for a while, he walked over to the shelves and began to poke around the dozens of neatly organized law and history books. All of a sudden, he noticed one that caught his attention: *Reality and Desire*. It was clearly his. This is my book. But what is it doing here? How did it get here? When did I buy it? He couldn't remember anything, other than the fact that it was, indeed, his. He knew full well which books he'd purchased throughout the years, which ones he'd read and which ones he had yet to read, and this one — he was certain — had never been opened.

With that thought he sat down on the edge of the bed. He turned on the lamp on the nightstand to his left, and opened the yellow-colored paperback to a random page. The first thing he found was a poem titled "Dead Child." Curious, not knowing what to expect, he began to read:

If the clear, fleeting voices of friends
Reach you there, under the grass,
Young like your body, already spreading across
An exile more expansive with death:
You think, perhaps, with a brooding nostalgia,
That your life is fodder for oblivion.

Perhaps you will remember our days together,
This letting go in the stream
Numb to labors and pains,
This slow, melancholy extinguishing,
Like the flames of your ancient hearth,
Like the rain falling upon that roof.

Perhaps you are looking for the fields around your village,
The happily galloping colts,
The yellow light upon the stone walls,
The old gray tower, one side in shadow,
Like a faithful hand will guide you
Through the lost paths in the night.

You'll remember crossing the sea one day
During your tender childhood with your friends
Blooming, so far away from the war.
Anguish slipped among you
And the sea darkened at the sight of your smile,
Unaware that it was the one that would carry you,
After a brief exile, to your death.

I would have shared those terse
Hospital hours. Your eyes alone
Facing the stern image of death.
Refusing to accept God's dream.
As fragile as your body may have been,
As vigorous and virile was your soul.

In a single swallow you downed
Your own death, destined for you,
Without a moment's glance back
Behind you, like a fighting man.
Immense indifference overwhelmed you
Before the earth finally sheltered you.

The tears that you yourself have not shed,
I will cry them for you. I didn't have it in me
To scare the death from you, as if it were
A vexatious dog. And how useless it is to want
To see you fully grown, green and pure,
Walking along as your other friends do
Through the clean air over the English countryside
In lively fashion.

You turned your head towards the wall:
The gesture of a child who feared
Revealing the fragility of his wish.
And the long, eternal shadow covered you.
Sleeping soundly. But listen:
I want to be with you. You are not alone.

39

When he arrived in London on that May afternoon, the first thing he did was look for Rafael Martínez Nadal at his flat in Queen's Court, not far from Kensington. As soon as Luis saw him there with his sister and mother (a life preserver in the middle of the ocean), he told them what had happened amidst a rush of tears which he couldn't hold back, despite the inner courage that had allowed them to flow. The three of them listened to him without saying a word, without any sort of interruption, completely astonished by the story of Sobrino. Rafael's mother brought out the teapot and served four cups of tea. She also fixed a cheese sandwich for Cernuda, who wolfed it down in a flash. That's how hungry he was. A short while later, Cernuda told them he'd written a poem to honor the child. Lola asked if he would read it. Luis took the three handwritten pages and began. Part way through, he felt himself getting short of breath, as if something far beyond his own power was taking over, preventing him from going on. But nevertheless he was able to finish the poem. When he was done, the four remained silent for what seemed like an eternal minute. None of them, not even Cernuda himself, knew how to react. Lola and her mother wiped away their tears with a handkerchief. Not only did the poem evoke Iñaki's recent past in Bilbao and his impossible future, but it also managed to convey Luis's present state of upheaval. Brimming with tenderness and compassion, this elegy on the death of a Basque boy was able to express the desolation felt by anyone who might be able to share in that pain, for it was, after all, about someone's son, someone's nephew.

Seeing him there, helpless, as discouraged as a thousand-year-old man, Rafael and Lola's elderly mother asked him if he would please stay with them until he was able to resolve his financial problems. They said "financial" problems but ultimately it was about all the other things afflicting Luis's body and soul: his longing for Spain, his anger, his shame, his disillusionment, his powerlessness, and, yes, his lack of money. Luis had no other choice but to accept her offer: he had nobody else in the world, no country, no home, no job, no money, no love to give nor any love to receive, and he didn't want to see Stanley Richardson, despite the fact that he knew perfectly well that sooner or later he would come knocking at Rafael's house, looking for him.

Before he left, Cernuda was to present Martínez Nadal's mother with his lovely elegy to José Sobrino. But first, he changed the title. Now the poem was called "Dead Child."

40

Luis sat there on the edge of the bed, awash in tears, not moving a muscle. *Reality and Desire* was lying face down on his lap, opened to the page where he found the poem he'd just read and which Cernuda had written eighty years before. He wasn't sure how long he'd been sitting here, petrified, shedding the tears of his grief drawn from his own well of bitterness. He didn't know the story behind "Dead Child," he didn't know who that child might have been, and he didn't even know if he had read any of Cernuda's poems before in his life, but still it was as if this poet from Seville had dedicated that elegy specifically to his newly-deceased nephew, or almost as if he, Salerno Insausti, had whispered it into the ear of Marcela's son, telling him that he wasn't alone either, that he wasn't fodder for oblivion, even while understanding the fact that he would never even see his fully grown body, green and pure.

Before closing the book, he happened to find, scribbled on the very last page next to the colophon, a phone number written in his own handwriting. Next to the digits was a strange name: Setefilla. Luis recalled that it matched the email address he had just received the day before, back in New York. But who on Earth had a last name like that? The more he tried, the more he failed to remember: he couldn't picture a single facial feature that would go with such a surname. One thing was clear, however: this person wanted to see his eyes again . . . But why?

Without a second thought, he grabbed the phone off the night-stand and dialed the number. It rang once, twice, three times:

"Hello?" said a woman's voice.

"Yes, hello . . ."

"Who's calling?"

Luis hesitated.

"Is this the Setefilla household?"

"No, it's not," the voice replied, also after a moment of hesitation.

"My apologies," Luis said, not quite sure whether he should hang up.

"Wait," said the voice on the other end of the line. "Who is this?"

"I must have the wrong number," Luis lied.

"This is Setefilla. There's no Setefilla household. Just me, Setefilla Rosas. Who are you?"

Hearing that name—rather, after hearing the first and last names together—Luis understood, he realized his mistake: Setefilla wasn't a surname, it was a first name. This wasn't about someone named Rosa. Apparently, he had just read what he wanted to read in yesterday's email.

"Who is this?" the woman insisted.

"Luis Salerno." As soon as he spoke his name, Luis regretted it. But the deed was done: she had given him her name, and Luis had given his as well.

"Luis?"

"Do we know each other?"

"Of course."

"Did you email me yesterday?" Luis dared to venture, still not entirely sure that he had correctly identified the voice on the other end of the line.

"Yes, that was me."

Luis wasn't expecting such frankness.

"So why did you say it was a mistake in your second email?"

"I was being stupid, I guess … Maybe because I was a little afraid."

"Afraid of what?"

"Afraid that you wouldn't remember me."

She was right: he didn't remember her.

"Do you know who I am?" Setefilla asked.

"Honestly, no."

"So I was right. See? You don't remember me."

Since Luis clearly didn't know how to respond, she added: "Why would you call me if you don't know who I am?"

"Because you emailed me first, saying you wanted to see my eyes ..." This, of course, was another lie. It wasn't the reason he had called, but it was the first thing that came to mind.

"So you do know who I am," she pressed.

"I'm sorry, but I don't," Luis said yet again.

"But you called me. You dug up my number and called me after all these years. I'm confused."

Luis hesitated yet again. How could he explain this coincidence? How could he tell her that he hadn't made the connection between the email and the phone number until thirty seconds ago?

He tried to fix his explanation: "Yes, but I called you to find out who you were, because I don't remember. I honestly don't remember where or when or anything else about where we met. I found your number completely by chance ..."

"By chance?" she laughed in an affable yet skeptical tone. "You call me exactly one day after I finally get up the courage to email you? I don't believe in chance, Luis ..."

Luis agreed that it was a bit unbelievable.

"Anyway, it doesn't matter," she continued, rescuing him. "I'm really glad you called. I would have been too nervous to do it myself, aside from the fact that I don't have your number."

"But you emailed me ..."

"Yes, but as you saw, a few minutes later I regretted it."

"That's the thing I don't understand, Setefilla ..." It was the first time that Luis had spoken that strange, unique name. "What's there to be afraid of? Me?"

"It's not exactly about being afraid. It's something else. It's a long story ..."

Luis couldn't help but recognize that expression: it's a long story, it's a long story. Amparo, his half sister, always said that when she was on the phone. It served only to heighten the mystery and to annoy the listener.

"That's okay," Luis said. "You don't have to tell me what you're afraid of. Just tell me where we met and who you are. My memory is so bad ..."

"I see that," Setefilla said. "Ten years ago. We met exactly ten years ago, can you believe it?"

"Really?"

"Yes, at El Péndulo in Polanco. Now do you remember?"

"No, not yet. I'm sorry …"

"You were there with a friend. I went up to you and said that I knew you, and later you came over to my table and asked for my number. You wrote it down in that yellow paperback you had. I remember it well. It was a book by Cernuda."

Finally Luis remembered. Of course he remembered that moment, and yes, many years had passed since then. He felt the burning desire to smoke, but he didn't have any cigarettes on hand. He should have better prepared before making the call.

"Women always remember the details …"

"I see that. Even the name of the book I wrote your number in. That's pretty impressive."

"Not really. Not as much as you might think," Setefilla was happy to say. "That book was the reason you caught my attention. Cernuda was a friend of my grandfather in Spain. I love Cernuda. And yes, of course I have that exact same edition of *Reality and Desire*. For years now, I've read it before I went to sleep. Since before I met you, even."

Luis was shaking like a leaf. He didn't know what to say, how to explain all this to Setefilla, how to explain himself.

So he made a joke, hoping simply to break the tension: "So it wasn't my eyes, then?"

"Actually it was those two things: your eyes, and the fact that you had a Luis Cernuda book. I'm a poet too."

Did that "too" mean that she thought he was a poet, or that she wrote poetry herself, as Cernuda did? It must be the latter, of course. Still, though, Salerno wasn't sure whether to explain the real reason he had that book: that Jacinto had told him to buy it on that distant morning, and also that, like she said, ten years had passed without him even cracking the spine of that book … until today. Yes, Luis thought, maybe she should have focused on Jacinto, the real poet, and not on me. Life can be ironic like that. But how could he say that now?

"You know, I actually go by Setefilla because of Cernuda."

"Really?"

"It's a long story."

Again with that same, strange expression.

"So why didn't we see each other after that? What happened?" Luis asked.

"Well, we did see each other. But you never called."

"I didn't?" Luis felt like a drifting ship, carried along by the waves, leading him across an ocean of forgetfulness. He had to believe everything that Setefilla Rosas was telling him because he simply didn't remember anything. It was enough, though, for her to resuscitate the memories, firing up the furnace in the basement of his subconscious mind, and finally his memory would sputter and start, resurrecting images and moments. His mother was right in one regard: his memory was like Teflon.

"You really don't remember, Luis?"

"I don't, I swear."

"We saw each other in Acapulco, almost two years after El Péndulo."

"Did you say Acapulco?"

"Yes, it was by chance, since you never called me. I thought you were going to call me after you came up to my table and asked for my number, but you never did. When I asked you at the club why you never called me, you said the same thing: that you forgot where you'd written my number. God you've got a bad memory!"

"At the club? Which club?"

"At the Palladium, almost eight years ago. Easter weekend, remember?"

When he heard "Palladium," all the memories from that distant, drunken night came rushing back into his brain. The word itself was like a flash, a detonation of everything that happened back when they would go looking for women, when he'd still courted or seduced or slept with women without regard for the fact that he might prefer some men more, without ever imagining that, many years later, he would have a Chilean boyfriend, and that after Alfredo, he would go on to sleep with three or four other men. And not only that: when he heard her say "Palladium," Luis recaptured the lost fragment of his dream in the taxi, the mysterious image of waking up in an unknown hotel room, washing his face, getting dressed, and leaving without ever seeing the person whom he'd been with. Yes, that was it: Setefilla wasn't with him when he woke up the morning or afternoon of the next day. Now he remembered. Not once during all those intervening years did he have a single recollection of that night in Acapulco, or of the massive hangover that dogged him the entire next day. These are things that you either forget about or choose to bury. Just another wasted night of partying lost among all the others, the dozens and dozens of others. Why would he ever have to remember it?

Hearing a prolonged silence instead of an answer, Setefilla said, slowly and seriously:

"Now do you remember?"

"Yes, more or less," Luis replied. "So what happened?"

"We never saw each other again."

"I mean, what happened to you? You weren't there when I woke up."

"I must have stepped out for something, because when I got back to the room you were gone. Vanished. It was all so strange, because I remember hearing you snoring right before I left. I remember it like it was yesterday, you know? You were snoring like a warthog. I thought to myself, 'That's what men do, Setefilla, what did you expect?'"

"Yes, I snore a lot."

"No, I'm talking about your disappearance," she said, laughing, before she dismissed the comment, and added instead: "I didn't have a lot of experience back then. I still don't, you know. A little more, maybe, but not much."

"I must have seemed like a complete asshole. I'm sorry," was the only thing he could think of to say.

"Don't worry. It wasn't your fault. That's what happens in Acapulco, right?"

"I guess so."

"I'd like to see you."

Luis froze. He should have expected something like that, of course, but the fact is that he hadn't even seen it coming, and he wasn't even remotely prepared for such a request. See each other? See her? Get together? His head was spinning. He really wished he had a cigarette so he could smoke, take some time, mull things over … He didn't know how he could explain his entire life to that woman, how he could describe how he felt, right now, over the phone, how he could tell her about the death of José, the pain that swept over him whenever he thought about his nephew. He also wanted to tell her that he hadn't lived in Mexico for several years, to tell her about the horrible reason for this quick visit, the heartrending event that had taken place, and which had nothing, absolutely nothing to do with her. But how to explain all of that? Where to begin? Could he get into all of this over the phone? Of course not. The last thing he wanted to do was offend her, especially after his disastrous forgetfulness, so much inexplicable disregard on his part. How to fix all of this? My God. How should he respond to this woman?

"But if you can't or don't want to, I understand, Luis. Don't worry."

"No, no," he lied. "Yes, of course, I'd like to see you too."

"There's more to the story."

"Well, considering we've only seen each other twice in our lives, you've already told me quite a bit, don't you think?" Luis smiled for the first time, chuckling at his own comment. "But yes, if you'd like, I can meet for coffee pretty much any day."

"How about tomorrow?"

He was trapped. Caught in a corner. He wasn't expecting her to be so eager to see him, especially after all those years. Why? To see his eyes again? It was ridiculous. He didn't even know if Setefilla was married or divorced or widowed, though that didn't much matter to him. On the other hand, she didn't know that he was gay, that he wasn't the same man he'd been before. Should he tell her now, preemptively? No. What good would that do? What purpose would that serve? He didn't know her; he barely even remembered her.

"Perfect," Luis said. "Tomorrow, then."

"How about the same place where we met? I live in the Irrigación neighborhood. It's close. We could have breakfast."

"At El Péndulo in Polanco, you mean?"

"Yes, they have great coffee there."

"Illy caffe."

"Illy, of course. At ten?"

"I'll be there," Luis said, before suddenly adding, to conceal his bewilderment: "I wonder if you'll think I'm very different."

"The same goes for me," Setefilla said, before immediately correcting herself: "But then again, you don't remember me. Your memory is like Teflon."

"I'm sure I'll remember you when I see you. I promise."

"We'll see . . ."

41

When he got out of the shower, Luis heard voices coming from the living room. He opened his suitcase and pulled out a pair of underwear and a clean shirt. He got dressed in a flash and decided to go downstairs to see who else had arrived at Marcela's house. From the stairs, he could see his parents sitting together, side by side, talking. Nobody else was there.

"We were waiting for you," his mother said, standing up and hugging him.

"I was in the shower, Mom."

"Yes, I know ..."

"Hi Luis," his father said, also getting up and taking a few steps toward him. Should he kiss him? Hug him? Shake his hand? This was all very strange: they'd seen each other here just a few hours ago, and yet they hadn't exchanged so much as a word.

"Hi Dad." They embraced. It was, however, a quick hug, lacking in warmth.

"How are you?" his mother asked, taking him by the hand and sitting him down next to her as if he were a little child. His father sat down in an armchair facing them.

"What can I say, Mom?" Luis replied cautiously. "Terrible. Awful. Really sad, like everyone."

"I can't believe it. I still just can't believe what's happened," his mother said, daubing her eyes with her handkerchief: evidently, she had been crying all night and on into the morning. "So you're going to mass, I suppose."

"I didn't know there was going to be a mass."

"At seven," his father said.

"I'll go." But that was a lie: he wasn't going to some mass. For what? If his sister needed to be consoled, he'd do it himself, here at the house. He wasn't going anywhere else. And if his own parents didn't believe in God, then why would they be having a mass? To deceive themselves? To simultaneously fool and alleviate their suffering souls? He'd rather not ask.

"You must be exhausted," his father said.

"I haven't slept at all."

"We haven't either," his mother said, squeezing his hand. "You look good, Luis. Have you gained some weight?"

"I think so, Mom."

"Tell us how you're doing in New York. How's everything going there?"

"Marcela isn't here," Luis said for no reason at all, other than to perhaps find a way to say goodbye to his parents so he could sleep all afternoon. He didn't want to talk. He didn't know what else to say. He felt empty, hollow, speechless.

"We know that," his father said. But the way he said it seemed to hint at something very specific, and Luis picked up on that. "That's why we're here."

"Your father wants to talk with you," his mother said, still holding his hand, and squeezing it even more tightly now. "Cirilo told us he dropped you off here."

Luis remained silent, confused but slightly intrigued: what could his parents have to say? Why had they come? They weren't here to see Marcela or Augusto or his nephew Fernando. That much was clear. They were here for him, to speak with him. And that's when he realized what it was all about.

"Dad," he said, his voice calm though resolute. "We can talk about ourselves some other time. I promise. I was thinking of staying here for a couple weeks," he lied. "We've got plenty of time."

"I'm not here to talk about the past, Luis," his father said, clearing his throat. There was a hint of fear in this tone, a strange note that Luis had never heard before. His father was speaking as if he had suddenly become some other person, as it were if some stranger was sitting there, muttering phrases. If they were talking on the phone, Luis wouldn't have recognized him. "I have cancer."

"What?" Luis wanted to believe that he had misunderstood, but in fact he had heard him quite clearly.

"Your sisters don't know yet. They don't know anything."

Luis felt paralyzed, breathless. He'd heard the word "cancer," and that was it. For a moment, he thought he was still in the midst of a very long dream, one that had started yesterday afternoon in Manhattan ... or even long before that.

"I'm the only one who knows," his mother said, suddenly and softly.

"Dad, how long have you known?" Salerno asked.

"About three weeks. It's everywhere. It started in my liver and metastasized to the pancreas. At this point, there's nothing they can do."

"Don't talk like that," Luis's mother snapped. The look in her eyes could have burned right through him. In those maternal eyes, Luis thought he could see a hint of pleading, of anger, and of pain, all mixed together.

"Are you sure?" Luis asked.

"I have six months. Maybe seven."

"But Dad, what about chemo?" Luis pressed, shocked and suffocated by the news. "You're not even going to try?"

"Your father has already started treatment," his mother explained.

"I'm doing it for her." His father grinned, though his voice still had that same muffled, muted tone. "But even so, I'm well aware of the fact that there's no cure. The oncologist was very clear during my last appointment."

"You have to try everything," Luis's mother said, admonishing him again.

"That's why I'm doing it," his father replied. Then, turning back to his son, he added: "I'd like for you to stay with me until the end. But if you can't—if you have to get back—I understand."

Luis began to cry.

42

Cernuda remembered that when he was a child he had possessed a blind religious faith. He wanted to do good deeds, not because he expected reward or feared punishment, but out of the instinct to follow a beautiful order established by God, in which the irruption of evil was as much a matter of dissonance as of sin. But into this childish notion of God was mixed insidiously that of eternity. And sometimes in bed, awake earlier than usual, in the early morning silence of the house, he was assaulted by fear of eternity, of time without end.

The word forever, applied to the consciousness of the spiritual being inside him, filled him with terror, which then became lost in a sense of dissolution, like a drowning body vanishing in waves of an oceanic flood. He felt his life attacked by two enemies, one in front of him and one behind, not wanting to go forward yet unable to turn back. This, if it had been possible, is what he would have preferred: to go back, return to that hazy unremembered region from which he had first come into this world.

From what mysterious depth in him did those thoughts spring? He tried to force his memory, to recover the consciousness of where, calm and unconscious, amid clouds of unknowing, he had been taken by God's hand and pulled into time and life. Sleep was again the only thing that answered his questions. And then that voiceless, unconsoling response was incomprehensible.

43

When Luis arrived at El Péndulo in Polanco, Setefilla was sitting there waiting for him with a cup of coffee in her hands. Luis recognized those green eyes as soon as they both noticed each other from a distance. It was so strange, though, to realize that ten years had passed since they'd first met in that very same place, if even for the blink of an eye: they were both the same, but ten years of life had (all at once) made them different people. And that was the odd thing, Luis thought as he walked up to the terrace where their small table was waiting for him. At what point do we cease to be what we were, and become something new, something distinct? How and why does that happen? Do we change with each passing millisecond? Are our lives an eternal succession of selves, a constant state of transformation ... from birth until death and on into the great beyond? Is there nothing to hold on to, nothing fixed and stationary in this world? Is everything flowing, changing, in a state of succession? Luis would know the answer — or part of the answer — in just a few minutes ... He would glimpse it when they greeted each other with a kiss on the cheek; when Luis asked for a cup of illy caffe and suppressed his desire to light up a cigarette; he would divine it when she began to speak, telling him all about her life up until the decisive moment when they'd met in this same place ten years before; Luis understood how everything in the universe is ever susceptible to change while listening to Setefilla's clear voice, he knew how things were being transformed with every passing second and with every word you heard, and how what we learn and discover changes our lives forever, how we cease to be the same from one moment to the next, when someone in a café suddenly tells us that we are parents, that we have a seven-year-old son, a perfectly beautiful little son whom you don't know, Luis, a son to whom I've finally told the truth. Yes, I told him that he has a father just like all the other children, and that he has the same name as he does. I finally got the courage to do that just last week ... But do you know how it all started, Luis? Do you know why I decided to talk with him and now with you? I suppose it all began a couple of months ago, in the park, when Luisito asked me: 'Mommy, do you think the birds wish they had arms? Do you see that little bird flying back and forth between the ground and its nest, each time with a new twig in its beak? You see that, Mommy? It must be hard not having arms and having to carry a twig in your beak all the time. The poor thing could save himself a lot of work if only he had a pair of arms, don't you think?' And I replied with the first thing that came to mind: 'Well the birds don't know, because they've never had arms. What about you? Do you wish you had wings?' And do you know what his answer was? Do you know what he said without even looking away from me? You're not going to believe this, Luis. He said, 'Sometimes I do, mommy. And sometimes I wish I had a daddy like everybody else.'

Charleston, SC, 2008-2010. Spring Hill, TN, 2014-2015.

Post Scriptum, followed by
the *Tabula gratulatoria*

"And we wanted to be men
without worshipping some god."
—Luis Cernuda

Cernuda spent several weeks in Queen's Court until early July of
1938 when, fed up with the immobility of his destiny, he decided
to return to Paris with what little money he had managed to save,
which was just enough to continue prolonging one of the most miserable periods in his life. He thought, of course, of returning to
Spain, once he had saved up enough money in Paris. But not only
was he unable to save so much as a cent, and not only did he hit
rock bottom in his bitterness and pain, but he would never set foot
on Spanish soil again. His friends advised against it: returning to
Spain was a death sentence.

A few weeks later, and thanks to Stanley once again, he got a job
at the Cranleigh College boarding school in Surrey, England. But
that is another story.

For my part, I came to know Luis Cernuda in the early 80s. I was
about fifteen at the time (the same age as José Sobrino Riaño when
he died). Back then, I would often visit a little bookstore in the El
Relox shopping center, which was owned and operated by a Chilean
expat living in Mexico. Directly across from this shrine, there stood
another: four theaters showing licentious movies which, a few years
earlier, back in the 70s, had been something quite different, though
still a sanctuary of sorts: the Mundo Feliz daycare center, where my
mother would take my sisters and me. In the tiny confines of that
place there on Avenida de los Insurgentes, I jumped from the Latin
American modernists to the Generation of '27, while at the neigh-
boring establishment, I was educated by Edwige Fenech and Sasha
Montenegro. Whenever I had some money in my pocket, I would
either sneak into the theater or buy a new poetry anthology. I inhaled

Pedro Salinas, Dámaso Alonso, Federico García Lorca, Rafael Alberti, Emilio Prados, Jorge Guillén, Vicente Aleixandre, Miguel Hernández, César Vallejo, and Pablo Neruda, among many others. However, as time went on, the dazzling light they had all once sparked in me began to cool, fading over time, until eventually it went out. Left in their place was a single faint, restrained, dignified light that continued to fascinate me, causing me to question my moral and human assumptions, and that was the voice of Cernuda. His tone was at once beautiful and severe. From the first line that you read, you know you're dealing with a poet who stands out from all the others. Cernuda seemed to be the only one who was upset with the world (the complete opposite of Guillén, for example). Very early on, I discovered that this poet from Seville spoke about those difficult, personal things which, to me, were ultimately important. Cernuda didn't hold back when it came to bringing to light (and out of the shadows) things that I felt concerned me intimately, and he did it with an extraordinarly formal beauty, but also with something that, at least to me, seemed to have the virtue of cutting right to the bone, the most delicate (or closed off) part of our conscience. It was this muted, stern, courageous tone that struck me every time I read him and which, however, I couldn't quite interpret. Cernuda denied the world (or the values of the world) while still keeping an eye on the things and beings that populated it. Reading him had a way of provoking in me the desire to read him again, and then to immediately meditate on what I had just consumed. But why him, why was Cernuda able to achieve this? I've tried several times over the past three decades to explain it, and all I've managed to do is stammer out a few responses that barely begin to even halfway address this personal mystery. There is a quotation from Cocteau that Cernuda often cited and which might help to at least partially explain my passion for his work: "Whatever they censure, cultivate it, because that's what you are." It's nearly impossible, we know, to try to follow that advice (or deed) without the risk of being lynched; however, Cernuda lived it to the letter. Hence his infamous life, and also the impregnable ethos and honesty of his work.

I think the first thing I wrote that was dedicated to him was back during those early years: a bad sonnet which I ended up publishing in my first poetry chapbook in 1984. Shortly thereafter, on the twenty-fifth anniversary of his death, I wrote a short tribute for the "El Búho" supplement of *Excélsior* titled "Luis Cernuda and Nazim Hikmet." Then, some years later, three distichs honoring Cernuda emerged, which my friend Fernando Fernández very generously published in his literary magazine. That was around the same time, in 2004, that I was writing my most ambitious novel, *Un siglo tras de mí*. In it, the poet Sebastián Forns meets Cernuda at UNAM in 1961, and he dedicates his dissertation to him and his work. His daughter, Silvana, ends the novel in Colorado, reading one of Cernuda's most famous love poems, "If A Man Could Say How Much He Loves." Finally, in 2002, marking the one hundredth anniversary of his birth, I participated in a panel on Cernuda in Cairo, along with another self-confessed Cernudista, the Valencian poet Francisco Brines. There I read a long essay which somehow sketched out part of what takes place in this novel, and which, in a sui generis way, needed to be finished off—or perhaps settled up—one day before I could sit down and start writing what is now *The Family Interrupted*. In "Ethos, verdad, forma, deseo en la poesía de Luis Cernuda," I argued that, since critics often differentiate between pre-Siberian and post-Siberian Dostoyevsky, we could attempt to do the same thing with Cernuda, starting with his arrival in England in 1938 and the creation of those beautiful poems that were collected in his first book of exile, *Las nubes* (1937-1940). Of course, this deeply elegiac book marks a point of inflection, a before-and-after: *Las nubes* is a milestone not only in Cernuda's work but also, perhaps, in all of Spanish language lyrical poetry. Nothing quite like it had ever been written before. Before Cernuda and his "Spanish elegies," poetry was something else. Of all the moments of bereavement that comprise *Las nubes*, "Ode on the Death of a Basque Boy in England" (or "Dead Child") becomes what I believe is the most definitive—and also the most painful—journey of his life, and *The Family Interrupted* intends only to continue (as far as fiction can) the task of telling the story of this crucial voyage in Cernuda's life, and thus *also of his poetry during those years.*

I have plagiarized and interpolated three of Cernuda's short prose poems into the body of this novel. Who could tell us something about his childhood or his thoughts on God better than the poet himself? Other than them, and the poems included in the story, I should mention the other texts that have helped me through my investigation: *Luis Cernuda. Vida y obra* by Emilio Barón Palma; *Luis Cernuda. Fuerza de soledad* by Jordi Amat; *Luis Cernuda: el poeta en su leyenda* by Phillip W. Silver; *Españoles en la Gran Bretaña,* by Rafael Martínez Nadal; *La resistencia silenciosa. Fascismo y cultura en España* by Jordi Gracia; *Una España escindida: Federico García Lorca y Ramiro de Maeztu* by Armando Pereira; *Luis Cernuda. Años españoles (1902- 1938)* by Antonio Rivera Taravillo; *La fuerza del destino. Vida y poesía de Luis Cernuda* by Eloy Sánchez Rosillo; *Rebeldía, clasicismo y crisis. Luis Cernuda. Asedios plurales a un poeta príncipe* by Luis Antonio de Villena; *La poética del hombre dividido en la obra de Luis Cernuda* by Vicente Quirarte; *Luis Cernuda. Escritura, cuerpo y deseo,* by Manuel Ulacia; the pioneering essay "La palabra edificante" by Octavio Paz; the autobiographical text *Historial de un libro* by Cernuda himself; and the excellent essays collected by Derek Harris en *Luis Cernuda: A Study of the Poetry,* and finally the two enormous collective volumes published to commemorate the centenary of his birth and edited by James Valender: *Luis Cernuda (1902-1963)* and *Entre la realidad y el deseo: Luis Cernuda (1902- 1963).*

My translator, Ezra Fitz, and I would also like to express our deep appreciation to Stephen Kessler, who graciously allowed us to use his translations of the Cernuda poems that have been worked into this novel. His collections, *Written in Water: The Prose Poems of Luis Cernuda* and *Forbidden Pleasures: New Selected Poems (1924- 1949)* are true works of poetry themselves.

In regards to the other story that makes up *The Family Interrupted,* I can only add that its true dedicatee (the heart of the book) is no longer with his parents, his brother or with me, but that it is him, however, who, without even realizing it, pushed me from beyond the grave to tell the story about the meeting between Cernuda and the Basque child after over a decade of having imagined it. Two years before my nephew was to pass away, Jorge Volpi called me at home to tell me the opposite; in other words, something I had truly *never* imagined: "Eloy, you have a half sister, and her name is Carmen." The rest is fiction.

Finally, I would like to thank Tomás Regalado, Antonia Kerrigan, Raquel Urroz, Margot Kanán, Pedro Ángel Palou, Rocío Martínez, Jorge Volpi, Ramón Córdoba, Marina Santillán, Raúl Carrillo Arciniega, Margarita Schmid, and Katya Skow-Obenaus for their careful analysis and thoughtful commentary, and—above all—for her meticulous reading and unconditional support, I thank my wife, Leticia Barrera Navarro, without whom this novel couldn't have been what it is.

FRANKLIN COUNTY LIBRARY
906 NORTH MAIN STREET
LOUISBURG, NC 27549
BRANCHES IN BUNN,
FRANKLINTON, & YOUNGSVILLE

ELOY URROZ is the author of *The Obstacles*, *Friction*, and *The Novelist's Wife*, forthcoming from Dalkey Archive Press, along with several other volumes of poetry and literary criticism. He was one of the authors of the "Crack Manifesto," a statement by five Mexican writers dedicated to breaking with the pervading Latin American literary tradition. Born in New York in 1967, Urroz is currently a professor at The Citadel in South Carolina, where he teaches twentieth-century Latin American Literature, twentieth-century Spanish Poetry, and Creative Writing.

EZRA E. FITZ's translations of contemporary Latin American literature by Alberto Fuguet and Eloy Urroz have been praised by *The New York Times*, *The Washington Post*, *The New Yorker*, and *The Believer*, among other publications. His own novel, *The Morning Side of the Hill*, was published in 2014 by 2 Leaf Press.